Twistin' Matilda

Jon Gray Lang

TWISTIN' MATILDA

This is a work of fiction. Names, characters, organizations, places, events and incidents are either products of the author's imagination or used fictitiously. Any resemblance to actual persons, living or dead or actual events is purely coincidental.

Cover Image by Tithi Luadthong

ISBN 978-1-7323305-1-1

Library of Congress Control Number: 2019917061

Jon Gray Lang

To Liv, thanks for your honesty and everything else that you've done to help me get this idea off the ground.

Jon Gray Lang

THE MATILDA SERIES
The Matilda
Twistin' Matilda
Black Matilda
Secret Matilda
Waltzing Matilda

Also, by Jon Gray Lang
Nun with a Gun: Town with No Name

one

In The Hole

Moments before Captain Kaplean's ship, the M33, materialized in the Pequiz system, the Waratah shot out into the night sky. Even though the battle above Ninguiz raged around the troop carrier, nothing could tear the joy from the heart of Luli Qing while the Avadora receded off into the distance.

Galena Chadov's body bobbed loosely in the copilot's seat as the little ship dipped and weaved its way through the wreckage left from the battle. Luli glanced over as light glittered on the jagged edge of the broken faceplate of the Lieutenant's helmet. Fear bit into her when she saw that the dark fluid had pooled in her friend's eyes, mouth, and nostrils.

"Probably in her ears, too," she

lamented.

Luli swallowed the lump in her throat and glared out the front port as she forced the troop transport to twist and jink around the fragments of a shattered hull. The only hope for the Lieutenant lay in making the rendezvous with the Matilda.

As the merchant ship slowly grew larger through the viewport, Luli cursed, "You better have that blasted crash net up or this is going to be one hell of a messy landing!"

With a quick slap at the attitudinal jet controls, the boat's entry vector jiggered just enough that it should line up with the freighter's hangar bay.

"Hail Major, full of grace! Please don't let me die in space!" her chant echoed in the comm as the Waratah slid past the tail end of the old trawler. A glint of light reflected off the metal threads that ran through the net, "Thank you ever so much, Tom!"

The blackness of space around the Waratah suddenly lit up as though a new star had been born right behind it.

"Mission accomplished! The bomb has detonated!" she cheered before a second eye-piercing brightness shattered the dark.

The shock wave from the explosion rocked the little ship and flung an immense slab of superheated metal toward it. What had once been a beam slammed hard into the hull. The yoke flew out of the cyborg pilot's hands and the transport tumbled into a corkscrew spin. Luli was pitched roughly into her harness, but the straps did their job and kept her in place. She was thrown once again when the Waratah slammed into the crash net and came to a relative, albeit floating, stop.

The pent up breath that she had held onto exploded through her clenched teeth. "Any landing you can walk away from is a good one, right?" she cackled like a lunatic at her comatose passenger.

Vibrations wracked the crash net in waves. Dread hit Luli hard in the chest as she looked out past the open hangar bay doors. A sickly rainbow of colors gushed outward like an uncontrolled oil spill in the vacuum of space.

Luli Qing crammed her eyes shut and gagged when a turbid glut of mephitis, that reeked of burnt fruit and molten copper, flooded her suit's air filters.

***

"Anton!" Captain Delahaye cried out. "Damn it, Anton, what just happened? Where in the bloody void are we?"

She glared through the bow port into the roiling madness that now surrounded her battered ship, the Matilda. Monstrosities from the darkest corners of nightmares littered the starless field. Thousands of the horrors encircled the carcass of the ancient space liner, the Avadora, like a maelstrom. Even though the enormous ship disintegrated slowly within a nuclear blast, some compulsion drew more of them to it.

At Anton's helpless shrug, Jacquie shoved Derain out of the way and keyed the engine room comm, "Barney! Did you jump us? Barney!"

Barney's voice came back, "The jump engine is cold, Jacq. I don't have any power routed to it right now." There was a long pause, "Does it look like we jumped?"

"Hell yes, it looks like we jumped! Can't you taste it?" she bellowed as her knuckles turned white from her grip. "Never mind. Figure a way out, damn it. We can't stay here."

"The engine's cold, Captain. I'll... I'll see what I can do. Barney out."

The comm went dead. Jacquie flung herself back into the pilot's chair as Derain Tiwi calmly pulled the star chart for Ninguiz up on the nav screen.

Anton Roane stared blankly out the bow port, transfixed by the view, "It's just coming apart out there." He scratched at his chin in thought, '*but it's happening at a funeral's pace.*' As the explosion continued to slowly blossom outward, he grinned, "I guess it's a good thing that those critters are too agitated to have noticed us."

"Not helping, Rabbit," Jacquie reprimanded. "Quit staring out the Gods-be-damned window and help me figure out a way to get out of this place. There's little chance we'd survive another fight with those... things."

Jon Gray Lang

"Looks like we're drifting away too," continued Anton.

Luli's voice burst over the comm, "Captain! I need help getting Galena to sickbay! She's not breathing and she's been deprived of oxygen for a long time now. I... I don't know if she's even still alive."

Without a word, Anton pushed himself up and disappeared through the open hatch of the bridge.

Jacquie closed her eyes and sucked in a calming breath, "Rabbit is on his way over, Lu. I'll need you up here as soon as you get her squared away. We have some serious problems of our own."

The bounty hunter glanced over at Jacquie, "Ask her how my ship is..."

The glower she leveled at Derain could've burnt holes through his skin, "Leave it, Derain. We have more important things to worry about right now." The Captain pressed her hands to her temples, "By the Gods, I need a drink."

***

Anton jogged into the airlock changing room and bounded over to the small window. He waited patiently while Luli struggled to get Galena's body through the airlock hatch. Once the lock had cycled and Luli had pulled her helmet off, he punched the hatch controls and hustled his way over to the Lieutenant's crumpled form. As the hatch clicked shut behind him, a dark viscous fluid sandwiched between Galena's face and her broken faceplate oozed toward him. He leapt back in surprise and careened off the wall.

"What the hell is that?" he shouted after he caught his breath. "Ohdowas protect us. Is she contaminated?"

Luli dropped her helmet from a squat position and slid back against the wall, "I don't know." Her tired eyes lit upon his troubled expression, "I really don't."

He struggled to regain his footing before he stared at her incredulously, "Have you lost your mind or something? What the hell were you thinking? You've exposed us! We might all be infected now!" He grabbed her by the shoulders, "We could die!"

Her eyes closed as her head drooped, "Obviously, I wasn't. I didn't know what else to do." She wrung her hands as she got up and checked on Galena, "Damn it, she still isn't breathing. We need to get her into a med tube as soon as possible." She looked around until she spied an unbroken helmet.

"I'll run the decontamination protocol on us. Keep your fingers crossed," Anton groused as he lurched over to the control panel.

Luli leaned against the bulkhead while the chamber filled with a neutralizing agent and then a pale gas. Anton fidgeted in place as the light spectrum ran through its steps before it gave the all-clear. The neutralizing agent always made him itchy.

The pale gas slowly filtered out of the airlock and the inner hatch unlocked with a loud thunk.

"That was a stupid move Lu, a stupid move. You, of all people, should know that better than anyone else on board," admonished Anton. "We're in the clear this time, but that was dangerous." He began searching through the cabinets that lay recessed in the walls, "Now where is the anti-grav stretcher?"

Luli pointed to a cabinet against the bulkhead near the outer hatch. She slowly straightened up and helped him get the genorg's body onto the stretcher.

His shoulders slumped as he engaged the anti-grav unit of the stretcher, "We've got a hold full of soldiers, Lu. They uh... they're not going to like this. We'll need to cover her face up or something or there'll be questions."

"Hold on. Let me get this helmet on her first." Luli popped the old helmet clips and it clunked loudly against the decking. She pulled the new helmet over the unconscious Lieutenant and clicked it into place, "Okay. Let's get her down there."

"We'll have to be quiet-like, okay?" Anton pleaded.

Luli gave a weary thumbs up and hit the hatch release.

two

Zwicky

The airlock tunnel from the M33 slowly unraveled to meet up with the hatch of the CBC Remus. Captain Kaplean crossed his arms and tapped his foot impatiently. In an effort to relax, he gazed out through the nearest viewport. Debris from the conflict glittered in the starlight as it traveled inexorably toward the planet below.

Once the tunnel seal clicked into place, he brusquely stepped inside and traversed the length of the shaft. A low growl rumbled from deep inside his chest when he was forced to wait for the other hatch to open.

A boyish fellow stood at attention on the other side of the hatch when it finally opened, "Munitions Officer Graeme at your service, Captain...?"

Jon Gray Lang

The visiting Captain dressed the young man up and down as he moved past him onto the deck of the Remus, "You may refer to me as Captain." He peered out past the inner hatch, "Now, where can I find your commander, Mr. Graeme?"

"Uh, if you'll follow me, sir. We are still in the process of cataloging the survivors."

Mr. Graeme felt the eyes of the gruff officer bore into the back of his head as if willing him to move faster. Rumor had it that this man commanded one of the new Special Ops vessels and everyone knew that dark things happened on board them. Needless to say, but Mr. Graeme did pick up his pace.

The tension between the two built as they passed other soldiers in the long corridor. Once they came to a right turn, a gulp escaped the young officer. He stuttered as he pointed, "She will be on the bridge, sir. This way."

Captain Kaplean grimaced and the young man's shoulders slumped in response. But he continued to lead his charge deep into the bowels of the Capital Battle Cruiser.

Unlike his own command, this vessel had been built with only one purpose in mind, war. The bridge would be located in the belly of this monster, entrenched under the heaviest armor. She was a large craft with what should be a standard contingent of fifty small fighters, five support craft, ten ground assault ships, and twenty shock troop carriers.

The Remus was definitely a beast, an incredibly powerful beast. The M33 was minuscule in comparison, but he did not relish the command of a vessel this large. With a crew that numbered in the thousands, it was difficult to keep track of who your people were. Prior to his current commission, he had served as a low ranking officer aboard a ship similar in size to this one. It was not a lifestyle he looked back on with fondness.

Mr. Graeme stopped in front of a heavily armored hatch which had a guard posted to each side. The young officer announced himself and was given the go-ahead. Once the hatch opened, he turned to the imposing man and waved him through.

Captain Kaplean stepped onto a bridge roughly three times the size of his own and strode directly to the woman in command. As he made his way toward her, the placement of six other guards throughout the command center caught his eye.

He pondered, "A little heavy on the security detail. I wonder why?"

Captain Ellsbeth watched surreptitiously as the mysterious Captain crossed her command center in a manner that showed he knew his way around. She quickly deduced he must have previously served aboard a similar craft. "Commander Shafar? You have the bridge."

Before she allowed the man to even introduce himself, she pointed him toward her ready room. She followed him in and waved him to one of the empty seats in the room. She stepped over to the small bar and asked, "Would you like a drink? The Major knows I need one."

He nodded as his eyes darted around the ready room. There were some personal elements here and there otherwise it was sparse in decoration. The single item on the expansive desk was a holo of a family. The mouths of the people in the holo smiled as they waved before the cycle repeated. As soon as she had finished pouring the drinks, he felt her eyes on him.

"So what can I do for you...?" she asked as she slid into her chair.

"My apologies," he stated. "I am Captain Kaplean. But it is best that you forget that I ever came on board." His fingers traced the side of the glass she had placed in front of him, "As for what you can do for me, Captain Ellsbeth? I only need to know where that freighter went."

"I don't keep tabs on Special Services, Captain. Isn't that your department?" Before he was able to interject, she continued, "I received orders that a ship would come to me with the needed nuclear warheads. Lo and behold, such a ship came. I tried to commandeer that boat for a last-ditch attack on the enemy's vessel. That vessel is now nothing but wreckage. And it's all because of that little freighter." She took a long pull on the glass before she set it down.

He inquired with surprise, "They had

nukes?"

"They most assuredly did. And for that, I am glad," she replied.

"Where did they get them? How did they get them?" he muttered under his breath.

A light smile graced her lips, "No idea, Captain Kaplean. That would fall under the need to know and I definitely don't need to know. Now, if I were to speculate, I would think that they would be in the employ of someone else in your department." She caught his gaze and held it, "So, the question you should be asking is, is your house in order? Do you truly know who you take your orders from?"

She pointed with her glass, to indicate outside the hull of her cruiser, "As for where they went? I gave them orders and they took them. The freighter went down to the planet to try and rescue those drone troops that we'd left to rot. The troop ship took a nuke to the remnants of that behemoth out there and destroyed the invader's access point. I would assume that both ships were atomized with the rest of the fleet." She poured another drink for herself and offered him a refill.

He sat quietly at first and stroked the lip of the still full glass. Eventually, he simply asked, "The one who announced herself, Lieutenant Galena Chadov? She went out to the enemy ship? Is that correct?"

"Yes, that is correct."

He took a long drink and set the

mostly empty glass back down on the desk, "And you just let them go?"

A tiny smile crinkled the corners of her mouth as she stared fixedly into his dark eyes, "Yes. I did."

She emptied her glass and set it down on her desk, then intertwined her fingers, "To keep their ship, they threatened to destroy mine even though I had them trapped in my hangar. Then when I had nothing to offer, they took the jobs I no longer had the staff for and barely the stomach to order my people to do." A sardonic grin lit up her face, "And with that I applaud them. I hope they're still alive, Captain. I really do. This ship owes them a debt." She looked pointedly at him, "The Consortium owes them a debt."

Captain Kaplean sat back and his left eyebrow quirked. He reached for his glass and took another pull from it, "It would seem we do. What can you tell me about them? Individually speaking."

Jon Gray Lang

three

Burial on the Presidio Banks

"Why is this stupid bed so hard to control?" Rabbit growled as the gurney pushed up into his grip.

Luli stabbed at the lift button while she and Anton struggled to hold the stretcher still; the process of getting Galena down the hall had been trying enough. "The gyro in one of the anti-grav motors is stuck," she replied.

The front end of the bed suddenly dipped to the floor and the back end shot up into the air. It slammed into the cyborg's hip and went into a hard spin. Anton yanked the front end upward to keep Galena's head from smacking against the floor. The motors whirred loudly as the stretcher picked him up off his feet and dashed him against the ceiling.

Jon Gray Lang

The lift dinged as it slid open. A corner of the gurney caught on the lift door and it whirled into Anton's chest. He threw his arms up as he fell backward and his hands caught the edge of the bed. He brought it under semi-control, "Hurry up and drag that end into the lift!"

Luli yanked on the gurney and tried to pull it in. It shifted heavily and crushed her hand in the door jamb. She cursed as she leapt back and then a strap on the stretcher blew apart in Rabbit's hand. The gurney crashed hard into the other end of the lift door and the corner inside tapped the close button.

"No, no, no!" shouted Luli as the door trundled its way into the bed.

The gurney went vertical and the lower half of Galena's body slid free. The sudden shift of weight sent the top crashing into the elevator ceiling with a loud bang. Anton roared as he shouldered the rest of the stretcher into the lift. The door closed silently behind him.

"I thought the whole point of these things was to keep the patient still!" Rabbit growled in frustration as he slapped at the stretcher. It began to slowly spin in a counter-clockwise direction.

"Well, she would be still if you hadn't broken the other restraining strap!" Luli snarled back. "Now calm down!" As the lift slowly made its way down past the third floor, she caught his eye, "Tell me again why the genorgs would want to kill her?"

Anton muttered under his breath, "How many times can I say the same thing?"

The sound of Luli's foot as it tapped against the grating echoed in the lift.

"All right," Anton replied. "From what you told me, the people of Ninguiz were mutated just like the crew of that cruise liner. The Consortium troopers are convinced it's an infection, probably caused by whatever the hell that muck crawling around inside her helmet is. They told us story after story how the contaminated would go through a rapid physical and mental change. Their skin would go ashen, the eyes turned black and they would look wrong... distorted. The ones that survived became uncontrollably violent. Nothing seemed to help them. So, they treated the afflicted in the same way a doctor disposes of a malignant tumor. They cut them down without a second thought."

His head leaned back into the wall, "There were bodies everywhere, Lu. And when we left, there were hundreds, if not thousands more of what used to be people running around." He stared hard at her, "I'm not sure the genorgs made the wrong decision."

Luli slumped into the corner, deep in thought, "We'll have to sneak her in then."

"That's what I've been saying this whole time," barked Anton.

His shoulder banged into the stretcher as he pushed himself free of the wall. The

Lieutenant's body tilted to the right while the left side of the gurney shot upward.

Rabbit remarked, "We've got to get her out of this damn thing before it kills all of us."

The lift doors opened up onto a crowded cargo bay. Field bedding was laid out in orderly rows on the decking in the otherwise empty cargo bay. A path had been left cleared from the lift to the med lab and all the way to the airlock on the starboard side.

Luli looked astounded, "There are so many of them..."

"Both passenger containers are loaded to bear, too," Anton whispered.

One of the troopers looked up and made eye contact. A blood-soaked bandage encircled her head and a splint sleeve covered her left arm. Luli broke eye contact quickly. The plas-glass doors to the sickbay parted and a couple soldiers half-carried a wounded genorg out to her bedroll. Luli and Anton took a deep breath and clutched the stretcher firmly between them. They stepped out of the lift and walked with feigned ease through the sickbay doors.

Once they were in the med bay, Luli asked, "Doc... is there an open med tube? We've got another wounded soldier here."

"Che ta, che ta," the machine replied as one of its many arms pointed to an empty unit far off in the corner.

A handful of troopers gave them a surreptitious glance as they walked past on their way back out to the cargo bay. Once the plas-glass doors slid shut, Luli dragged the stretcher toward the corner. Rabbit cracked the lid of the med tube and with a practiced motion, they slid Galena inside. Luli quickly popped the helmet release and slammed the lid shut. While Anton dealt with syncing the module up to its patient, Luli sidled over to the automaton and tried to gain its attention.

"Doc. Doc, I need you to listen," she demanded.

Doc's multifaceted visual assembly glinted in the overhead lights as it spun toward her. It made a querying noise while it kept working on the patient that lay on the examination table.

She waited until the assembly unit stopped moving and grabbed it with one hand, "This is very important." She pointed over to where Anton stood, "That patient is extra special. She is more than one of the soldiers, she is part of the crew, understand? So, please keep an eye on her."

"Shi lo da? Es ed to do!"

Luli grumbled, "I understand that they are all your patients. But I need you to be extra sure with that one. That's all." She waited a moment, "Got it?"

"Ed to do, che da!" it harrumphed as its visual assembly rotated back to the current patient.

"Thank you, Doc. Always a pleasure." She rolled her eyes and met up with

Anton at the comm panel. She keyed the comm to the bridge, "Captain? We are on our way back up. Be there in a few."

***

By the time Anton and Luli made their way back to the bridge, Barney had beaten them there. He threw a small wave in their direction before he went back to what he had been working on at the nav console. From what Anton could see, the engineer was comparing readings from their current location to those taken from the recently vacated Pequiz system. Jacquie quickly glanced up from her conversation with Derain before she leapt over and enveloped Luli in a big hug.

"Gods, am I glad you're back, Lu. You have no idea how happy I am to see you." The hug lingered a bit longer before she sank back into her chair. Her hands roughly gripped the armrests, "First off, how is our Lieutenant?"

A raucous screech trumpeted from beyond the ship and the bulkheads shook in response. Tension filled the bridge as something large brushed against the skin of the freighter. No one moved a muscle until only silence remained.

"I cannot wait to get away from that," muttered Derain.

Luli shook herself while she gathered her thoughts, "Galena's not good, Jacq. We were waylaid by a gang of those creatures on that ship of death." A questioning look lit up her face, "By the way, does the name Avadora ring a bell to anyone?"

Barney shook his head while Derain shrugged in response.

Her eyes slid over to the bow port before she continued, "Her helmet faceplate got crushed during the fight. I had to drag her ass out of there and the run back to the Waratah felt like forever. Her helmet was no longer airtight, so..."

Anton interjected, "Will you get to the bad news already?"

"I am getting to it, damn it!" she shouted. "Anyway, one of those horrors tried to eat her. I pulled her free from its mouth and the monster's blood or whatever stuck to the exposed skin. I... I tried to scrape it off, but it just slithered away from me. With the bomb set, time was of the essence so I hauled her back as is." Disappointment radiated from her, "Anton thinks she might be infected like the people on that rock. I'm hoping Doc can figure out how to get it off of her."

Jacquie pinched the bridge of her nose as her eyes tightened, "Mostly black in color, like tar?" Luli's nod confirmed her fears. "Does she look different? Disfigured?"

"Not yet," muttered Anton.

Derain's voice broke in, "Those drone soldiers are going to kill her and probably us as soon as they find her."

"Hey! We got her in the med tube without any of them questioning what we were doing!" Anton shot back. "We should be in the clear for now."

"Until the tin-can makes its medical report, you mean," retorted Derain.

Jacquie sucked in a breath, "We'll deal with that when we have to." She pointed out the window, "Luli? I'm going to need you and Barney to figure out a way to get us away from that."

Luli stepped over to the bow port and her eyes grew transfixed. The roiling madness of the sky was stranger than it had been on their last journey through 'other space'. A feeling, that if she watched long enough a burgeoning pattern could be seen interwoven through it, struck her. But it was difficult to observe, so its appearance remained erratic. She tracked to where the ship she had blown up should have been and surprise hit her hard. It was still mostly intact. The Avadora continued its eventual decay in slow motion.

"It's still out there?" she blurted out. "How is that even possible?"

"How is any of this possible? How did we end up here?" Jacquie's hands curled into fists, "But what I really want to know is how do we get back to our own space?"

Derain cleared his throat, "I've been watching them for a while now and I think Anton may be on to something. The Avadora's destruction has them too preoccupied to bother with us. Which means we have time to prepare. But how much time do we have before they do take notice of the

Matilda?"   A gut-wrenching hoot suddenly penetrated the hull and everyone grew quiet again.

Barney looked up from his charts and wiped a hand across his brow, "Well, I think I've figured out how we got here."

Luli padded over to the empty pilot's chair and slipped into her seat. Anton shuffled disconsolately out of the way.

The crew grew quiet while Barney reported, "From the sheer number of wave distortions radiating outward, it looks like that rift had been open for a long time. Long before we got there. Maybe even long before the Consortium was notified to try and contain it." He shrugged, "It's hard to tell."

Derain shifted in his seat as Barney continued, "From everything I've been able to cobble together, that fissure was caused by something that runs on the same principle as our jump engine. But it must have had an enormous power source to keep it open and immobile for that long."

Luli jumped in, "That fits. We came across another jump engine over there. It was easily three times the size of ours. Weirdly enough, the ship itself seemed to be coming apart at the seams. It was like the engine rooted the Avadora to that point in space against all the gravitational forces coming from both sides of the rift. Somehow, she remained intact even as she was being torn apart."

"That fits with my thinking," Barney

murmured. "With that engine running for such a prolonged time, the walls between the two dimensions weakened until they became thin... paper-thin. So thin, that it's my belief that we just fell through."

His somber eyes looked up at the Captain, "I still don't know how we're going to get back. We usually use two linked points in our space to set the destination. But starting off here with no idea where here is in relation to anything in our space? It's all guesswork at this point."

Luli crossed her arms, "I was able to get some readings from that big engine directly. Maybe that'll help?"

"Can't hurt." Barney chewed on the end of his finger in thought, "Captain? If you'll excuse me and Ms. Qing, I'd like to get a start on what she brought back."

"Don't let me stop you," replied Jacquie. "The sooner we're out of here, the sooner we can relax."

The comm panel lit up and the familiar voice of a genorg came over, "Captain? This is Delta 555-74K. We have matters to discuss with you. When could we meet?"

Jacquie keyed the comm back as Luli and Barney stepped out, "Meet me in the gym. I'll be there in a few minutes."

"We look forward to speaking with you. Delta out."

Derain muttered into the quiet, "That

sounded ominous."

Jacquie rubbed her temples before she addressed the two men, "You two have the bridge. Tom knows I could really use a drink right now."

After she disappeared around the corner, Anton poked Derain, "Have you got a deck of cards on you? Got a feeling this is going to be a long day."

four

Maps

Jacquie stood with her arms crossed as she rode the lift down. She barely waited for the doors to part before she stepped out onto the second deck. Two fully armed guards were posted outside the hatch to the gym. They kept an eye on her as she stopped to straighten her vest and brush back a few strands of her hair before she moved past them.

The lighting in the gym was maxed to almost glaring but it was preternaturally quiet. This struck her as odd simply due to the fact that there were two troopers waiting for her. They stood stock still in the very center of the room. Their lack of movement and sound made the situation a bit eerie.

"Delta? Is that Gamma with you?"

Gamma's expression melted from its

Jon Gray Lang

stoic mien to a shy smile that brought to mind Galena. It was a bit disconcerting, but in a way, it was also comforting.

"That is correct, Captain," Delta replied. "To be honest, I am surprised and impressed that a natural born such as you is able to recognize us individually."

Jacquie's eyebrows quirked a little before she answered, "Well, it's mostly due to the wear and tear of your uniforms. Galena once remarked that being recognized as an individual was one of the kindest sentiments that a person could do for her. So I try. But, we're on a tight schedule, so if we could get down to the business at hand?"

"Of course," replied Delta.

"Now, what is it that I can do for you? You and your sisters, that is." Jacquie moved over to the weight set and slipped onto the bench, "Pull up a pew if you can find one."

Gamma scanned the gym absently before she settled to the decking in front of the Captain. Delta sidled up next to her sibling.

"Who did your crew bring on board and have stowed in a med tube?" asked Gamma. "The life sign readings on the med tube are... odd. Should we be concerned?"

Jacquie glumly stared at the two women on the floor as she clasped her hands, "The patient is a member of my crew. She was injured during the assault on the enemy fleet."

"Is she Lieutenant Chadov?" Delta

inquired. "We are aware that the First Soldier remains unaccounted for."

Jacquie blinked a moment before she nodded in ascent.

The relief from the two genorgs was palpable as they spoke in unison, "We are pleased to hear that she endures."

A chill ran down the Captain's spine. "To be honest, she's in a bad way. We... uh... we're doing everything we can to get her through this, but she may not make it." A thoughtful look crossed her face, "But thank you. I think she would appreciate your concern."

"Our people are normally left to die where they fall. It is fortunate that she has forged a bond with you natural-borns. This may be an unprecedented feat," replied Gamma as she threw a side glance to Delta. "Please keep us informed as to her condition."

Delta squeezed Gamma's shoulder until the other genorg quieted.

"Lastly, are we under your command?" Delta asked. "If so, do you have any orders for us, Captain?"

Jacquie joked, "Now, what would I do with an army of genorg troops? I mean, what else can you do with just shy of four hundred soldiers, besides take over a city or a whole moon?"

She cleared her throat at their unchanging demeanor, "Well um... No, we didn't receive any orders for you. You're not under my command." Jacquie threw her hands in the air, "I guess your lives are your own now. What would you and your sisters like to do? Where would you like to go?"

Their faces blanked in confusion before they turned to each other and shared a quiet conversation. It quickly came to an end, but they just shrugged their shoulders in response.

With their lack of an answer, Jacquie deliberated a moment before she said, "We'll work on that later. Now, there's only one other bit of news I should bring to your attention and it's going to sound a bit mad."

She sucked in a big breath and let it out in a whoosh, "Currently, we're stuck somewhere outside of our universe, or it might be inside. We don't really know. Either way, we're working on a solution to get us all out of this."

A shriek exploded outside the hull of the Matilda and Jacquie winced, "And away from that."

"Thank you for letting us know, Captain," they replied in concert. "We appreciate the candor."

***

It had taken a thorough search of the bridge before Derain discovered a ragged deck of cards stuffed under a corner of the nav station. It wasn't much longer before he and Anton were deep into a game of poker.

"I'll call," Anton said as he threw in. "So, do you think we have a beggar's chance of getting out of here?"

"If anyone can find a way, it's those two. I'll raise you," Derain replied. "Barney and Lu know more about that freakish contraption and how it interacts with this place than anyone else."

"Well, anyone besides the Captain of the S.S. Kaboom out there. What did Luli name it, the Avadora?" muttered Anton.

"Yeah, that's it. I call it."

Anton grinned as his flush took the round. "The name familiar to you?"

"Not to me. I never paid too much attention to transport names unless they were harboring a skip I was after." Derain shuffled the deck, "This boat has been around for a long time. Why don't you have the Matilda run a search through her records?"

"Might as well. I'll have to find something else to do after I take the last of your mazuma," Anton winked.

"Har, har." Derain laid out the next hand, "Hole cards are dealt, four of clubs is on the table."

Anton plugged away at the ship's database and waited on the ping to let him know it had begun.

"Just do a search with an auto dump when it's done, alright?"

Anton spun around and rubbed his hands together, "Done. We've got a game to play and I'm feeling lucky."

Derain laughed, "Ah ha! That's your problem right there. Those kinds of feelings only lead to failure."

"Your failure and my winning, you mean," Anton joked.

A message alarm tripped the comm. Derain slid over to it and pulled the message. He read it once, then again. "Rabbit, come here and have a look at this."

Anton put Derain's cards back down, "Who's it from?"

"Doc finished its preliminary report on the drone... I mean the Lieutenant." He looked quizzically at the man, "Have you ever known that bot to be wrong?"

***

Luli and Barney were clustered together at the large table in the lounge. The ship's computer collated the scans Luli had collected aboard the Avadora against the readings from their own jumps. The table's screen grew brighter when Barney dumped in the current feed from the outside.

"That thing was pumping out a lot of power to keep that breach open, never mind the constant drain to keep it stationary!" Barney gestured at one of the entries, "Take a gander at

Jon Gray Lang

these energy levels. That would leave the Matilda here high and dry in minutes! You didn't happen to see what the orb using for power, did you?"

"We were in a pretty big hurry. Be lucky you got anything at all." Luli grew pensive, "I just hope the time it took to get them isn't the death of her."

"Doc's giving her a thorough going over, Lu. She's strong. She'll come out of it."

"I don't know, Barney. You didn't see what was happening to that ship... or what was left of the people on board."

"We saw some crazy stuff down on the planet's surface, too. The locals were definitely mutating into something. How and into what, I have no idea. Don't think I want to either," he shivered at the memory.

The external survey from the ship caught his eye. He flipped between it and the Pequiz system readings, "Luli, check this out!"

Derain's voice rang over the comm, "Captain and crew, please head to the lounge for a quick meet-up."

Luli flipped the comm on, "We're already here, Derain. What's up?"

"We're on our way to you. Have either of you seen Jacq?"

***

"What couldn't be said over the

comm, Derain?" Luli asked.

The bounty hunter glanced over at Anton who just cleared his throat and looked the other way.

"One of you spit it out," snapped the Captain. "Things are bad enough as is. We don't have the time for this hemming and hawing garbage. What did you call us together for?"

A large, scaled body scraped against the hull of the ship and the echo reverberated through the lounge. Tension filled the room as they all glanced toward the viewport and then back at each other.

Anton cleared his throat again, "Um, we've got Doc's medical report on the Lieutenant. That crud is inside of her now. It's moving through her bloodstream and Doc hasn't been able to peg down what it is or how to get it out of her. The really strange part is it's choosing where to go, like something alive."

At the disheartened looks, Derain countered, "But it's not all bad. The piece of tech embedded in her brain is regulating the contagion. It's keeping it in check."

"What do you mean keeping it in check?" asked Barney.

Anton shrugged, "That's the thing. Doc doesn't understand it either. The junk keeps attacking her blood cells or trying to bind with her at the genetic level, but the chip just shunts it somewhere else in her body. It can't get a solid foothold."

"We still have time to figure out what we can do for her," Jacquie surmised. "She's not a lost cause then."

"You have no idea how relieved I am to hear that," Luli declared loudly. "Well, let's all keep our seats on the good news train. Barney and I think we might have found a way out."

"It's a possibility," Barney hedged.

Luli continued, "Our best theory for what happened is that we fell into this 'other space'. The rift was open long enough that the wall between the two thinned and with all of the jumps the Matilda had done previously, she just kind of slipped in."

Anton jerked in shock, "So we wouldn't be here if she'd never made a jump? Even if we do get out of here, we could fall back through?"

Barney grunted, "She'd been used for jumps long before any of us came on board. There's a good chance we would've fallen through anyway."

"So bad news on top of bad news," groused Jacquie. "I don't think this qualifies as keeping our seats, Luli."

"But there is a good side to this!" Luli protested. "This means that the Matilda can essentially fall through another weak spot. And we're already working on tracking one."

"Why don't we just jump? What's the

worst that could happen?"

Luli's lips pursed, "Come on Anton, I know you're smarter than that. Sure, we could jump, but without a fixed originating point, we might never come out of it."

"Even if we were lucky enough to come out of it, we still might get sucked into a star or end up inside of a planet." Barney stabbed his finger at the table, "We're alive now. Nothing wants us dead at the moment. Let's see if this works before we go all last resorts, alright?"

An enormous appendage slapped wetly against the view port in the lounge and everyone jerked back in surprise. A huge, protuberant eye slid into view and glared at them.

Jacquie's voice quavered a moment before she ground out, "Well, get it done you two. There isn't a whole lot of sand left in our hourglass."

five

More Heat Than Light

A slight smile flickered across Captain Kaplean's face once he was finally back on board the M33. A formal stiffness faded from him as he made his way back to his ready room. By the time he had made himself comfortable, there was a knock at the door.

Yeoman Fitzpatrick entered, "Reporting for duty, sir. What do you require of me?"

The Captain appraised his third class petty officer. He was still a young fellow; good at his job, but not overly ingratiating. It did make him wonder what the young man had done to be enlisted into the Special Services branch. There were always reasons. But other things had precedence. Now was not the time to bother with an answer to that

Jon Gray Lang

question.

"Mr. Fitzpatrick, please pay attention. I need you to run searches on the following physical descriptions." The Captain pulled up the notes on his data pad, "This will be for a total of three persons. All of them lie somewhere between their early twenties to early forties, but as we're all aware, time dilation can make a mockery of this. Are you prepared?"

Once he received an affirmative nod, "The first one is female. Build runs to the mesomorph; roughly one hundred seventy centimeters in height with straight black hair and golden eyes. Skin tone falls toward medium brown. Introduces herself as Captain of the freighter we've been tracking. Still no name on file for her or the ship."

Yeoman Fitzpatrick furiously typed the information into his data pad, "Ready, sir."

"The second one is male. Also a mesomorph build but leaner. Roughly one hundred ninety centimeters in height with dark wavy hair and brown eyes. Skin tone falls between dark brown to black." As he perused his notes again, the curl of a smile appeared, "Actually from what Captain Ellsbeth told me, he and I have similar complexions. Once again, no name on file, but the profession is Bounty Hunter."

"Got it," replied Fitzpatrick.

"The third one on the list is also a male. Ectomorph build; roughly one hundred eighty centimeters in height with straight black hair and blue eyes. Skin tone falls between light to medium brown. Profession is unknown, but the individual goes by the moniker Rabbit."

"Sir? Isn't that the alias of the escaped convict from the Vogelgesang?" Fitzpatrick flipped through the screens on his data pad, "Umm... the terrorist? Where is he... Ah! Anton Roane?"

Captain Kaplean replied, "Yes, that is correct. Go ahead and strike that last one from the list. See what you can find about the other two."

"If I may speak freely, sir?" After a short nod from the Captain, "There isn't enough information here to run a proper search. Was there anything else that might help? Like scars, tattoos or other physical markers?"

The Captain brooded a moment, "Captain Ellsbeth didn't mention anything of that sort. The only other item that she brought up was that the trawler had a female pilot. She wasn't seen by any of her people and didn't have a recognizable accent." His eyes bored into the young officer, "Always remember that information, even a finite amount, is better than nothing, Yeoman."

"Sir, yes sir! I'll get started on this right away."

After Mr. Fitzpatrick left the ready room, Captain Kaplean settled back into his chair. His fingers knotted then unknotted in quick succession. "We're not quite back to square one, but we're not far off."

***

The Copperhead slid through the shipping traffic in the Erebus system on its way toward the planet Mithuna. The freighter was still loaded with most of the goods it had received from the Matilda only a couple weeks ago, ship time. Captain Ariel Kahn had already synced up her berth at port. For a change, the Loader's Union were ready to unload the goods and deliver them to the various waiting parties without delay. Somehow, she knew that Mr. Leon was responsible for this and she was glad of it. It was a boon not having to wait while the cargo rotted in her ship's hull.

Every time Mr. Leon came to her mind, somehow, like magic, he would appear shortly thereafter. He had been a passenger on her ship for so long that she had become inured to these little surprises.

"Good morning, Ms. Kahn," he said as he stepped through the hatch onto the bridge proper. "I see that we are set to arrive on Mithuna soon. There wouldn't happen to be any messages waiting for me, would there?"

She turned to regard the relatively nondescript man as he stood politely to the side with his hands behind his back. He smiled serenely while he gazed back at her and then out of the bow port of her vessel. She threw a questioning eye to Siede

Geist, who manned the comm station. Siede's head shook in the negative.

"We haven't received anything yet..." started the Captain.

Siede suddenly interrupted her, "Ariel? I just received a priority message for Mr. Leon. Should I accept?"

Ariel raised an eyebrow at him as a grin touched her lips, "Please do, Siede. Please do."

"I'll take it in my cabin, Ms. Geist," Mr. Leon stated as he left the bridge.

Siede glanced over at Ariel, "How does he do that?"

***

As Mr. Leon entered his cabin he found the other Mr. Leon, with the given name Rex, finishing the message. He quietly closed the hatch behind him before he asked, "What news do we have? And is it good?"

Rex looked up at his duplicate and positively beamed, "The ordnance delivery to the Pequiz system was a success."

"Oh, excellent news. Are there any details to be had or must I beg?" an amused Mr. Leon asked.

"Why, but of course there are details!" the other replied in a grandiose manner. "And no begging is required. Per the Captain of the CBC Remus, the rift has been closed and the alien menace thwarted."

Mr. Leon rubbed his hands together, "That is wonderful news. Any word on the Matilda?"

"Sadly, there is nothing regarding her. She simply vanished as the rift closed." He looked conspiratorially toward his compatriot, "Apparently another ship arrived in the system in search of our little freighter. And would you know, it was one of those new M Class light destroyers?"

"My, that does sound strange," Mr. Leon murmured in response. "What could the Special Services branch of our fine and upstanding Consortium government want with a small merchant vessel, I wonder?"

"Perhaps we should look into it."

"Perhaps we should." Mr. Leon pursed his lips, "I wonder who could possibly use a donation to their personal interests?"

"Or suddenly fear the loss of a valued family member?" followed Rex.

Mr. Leon grinned widely, "Maybe there is a connection to those soldiers who stormed our operation on Zangspur."

"One never knows..."

"... until one tries."

six

Dream On

Galena struggled to pull herself free from the blackness of oblivion. Her eyes cracked open only to find herself trapped on board the antiquated Avadora. While everything was dim and hazy, she could still make out the hall as it stretched off in both directions. Oddly, she was able to see through the walls closest to her. But they only showed her other hallways in the ship that stretched forever outward.

For some reason, her body wouldn't move. She strove to get an arm or a leg to respond. But they refused to obey her, no matter how hard she wished it. The decking underneath her felt strange as well. It was both rigid and fleshy, like fat over bone. When she looked down, fear tore at her mind. Her bones had become entwined with the deck plates and it was her organs and skin that lay puddled around her.

Sudden panic made her scream out and her body bucked violently. Her eyes squeezed shut to block the horror from her sight while her breath tore raggedly from her throat. The temperature dropped to freezing and what remained of her above deck shivered in response. Her eyes snapped open at the sudden change and the engine room of the Avadora surrounded her.

She whispered, "What is happening to me?"

Her movements were hampered as she struggled to turn around. From the corner of one eye, she could barely make out Luli as she set the timer for the bomb. Between them lay a body splayed out on the deck, but the face was partially obscured behind a broken faceplate. She recoiled in revulsion as she watched a black, viscous fluid run into the eyes, mouth, and nose of the face.

A thick fluid rushed down her throat and she struggled for breath. Her ears rang with the sound of her choking until the sensation dwindled. Tears cut tracks into the dirt smudged into her face as she watched Luli pick up the body and run through the hatch. She tried to cry out to her friend that she had taken the wrong one, but it was too late. A searing pain burned in her belly and she crumpled into the fetal position.

The rush of pain left as quickly as it arrived. Dry heaves shook her as she watched Luli

Jon Gray Lang

float overhead with a limp body strapped across her back. Galena's eyes were drawn to the dark ooze as it writhed across the face under the shattered faceplate. Her vision clouded over and she lost consciousness.

A stabbing pain jerked her awake. She was still imprisoned aboard the ship, but now she and the walls were one. Her eyes moved to and fro, but they ached from the strain. Feathery-like fronds that darted from her pupils tickled her cheeks as they reacted to a wind only they could sense.

"What is happening to me? What is happening to me? What is happening to me?" Galena cried out and thousands of voices echoed her loudly in her skull. She wailed until the anguish pushed everything back into oblivion.

***

Barney scratched at his forehead in consternation, "Luli, will you take a look at these? I can't get these sensor readings to make any kind of sense."

Luli replied, "Sure, let me finish this first... wait a minute. Wait a minute! Barney, get over here right now!"

Barney perked at the excitement, "What have you found?"

"Oh, come see it for yourself!" she yelled as she dragged him over to the simulation. "If you look here and here, you'll see that the

Matilda picked up speed right after slowing down."

His eyes widened in understanding, "That would mean..."

"That we're caught in a gravitational eddy," finished Luli. A grin broke out on her face, "We're being pulled toward something."

"And that can only be another weak point between the two realities!" cried the engineer as he swept Luli up into a hug.

"We've got a way out of here! We've got a way out of here!" the two of them sang as they bounced around in a circle.

Luli whispered, "Should we tell them?"

"Who's stopping you? Not me," giggled Barney.

Excitedly, Luli mashed the comm button, "Attention. Attention. I just want to inform everyone that we might have a way out of this place. Now don't get too excited because the when of it is still up in the air. Luli out."

She dropped the comm and spun over to Barney, "We've got a way out of here?

Barney smiled and nodded, "We've got a way out of here."

***

"That's great news, Lu!" Anton clicked the comm off and quick-stepped to the lift. This would be the third time in the same solar day that he had made his way down to the med lab but he felt the need to share the good news with Galena.

He wandered past the genorgs in the cargo bay, through the plas-glass doors. Once inside, he glided by the stacks of med tubes, each with its own occupant, until he spied the one that contained Galena. The small crate that he had been using as a stool slid into his hand as he sidled up next to it. With a sigh, he leaned against the wall of the med tube and meditated quietly for a time.

With his eyes still closed, he spoke softly against the shell of the tube to the comatose patient inside, "Doc told me that you can't hear me, but I'm not entirely sure I believe that. I mean, he doesn't really understand what's happening to you. Or if you're still you. I believe that you are." He glanced wistfully away, "Anyway, I just wanted to let you know that we might get out of this god's forsaken stretch of space."

He fiddled with his fingers before he continued, "I never expected to see you again, you know. In fact, I never wanted anything to do with you ever again. But that's all changed. I don't like seeing you like this." He stared down at her through the small window, "You surprise me. You've surprised me since I first met you on Tigron. You were such an enigma. I mean, a genorg on the battlefield? Not just on the battlefield but in command? What happened to put a genorg in charge?"

***

Galena caught the edge of a faint voice that seemed to come from a vast distance. She could barely make out the words, but it sounded like it was addressing her; talking to her. "I'm right here!" she cried out, but the voice kept on speaking as if it hadn't heard her.

Her eyes squeezed shut and hot tears rolled down her cheeks only to splash against the cold metal that rested against her jaw.

Only her head and shoulders remained above the decking in the engine room as more of her torso had slipped further down. The voice, Rabbit's voice, continued speaking just on the edge of her perception. She strained to listen; to hear what was being said. But the voice grew weaker, like the distance between them was growing.

The engine room rippled and wavered before her. The jump engine phased into focus and pulled her gaze toward it. Its turbid lights and fluctuating patterns captivated her. Something within it called to her and she could no longer look away. Anton's voice grew muffled and indistinct. She forced herself to focus on his words, but a deep throbbing cadence pounded into her brain. Her vision grew dazzled by the machine until she could no longer focus on anything else.

The remaining control she had over her physical form disappeared and the decking slowly knit into her shoulder blades while it pulled her down.   Pain exploded from her chest, then quickly bled away as she grew detached from the sensation.

Fear laced the words from the voice, but she could no longer understand the words nor remember who spoke them.   Her mind wandered while the throbbing in her skull flowed to match the patterns that played on the surface of the engine. Galena barely noticed when she sank completely into the floor.

***

The alarm on Galena's med tube squawked loudly over the hushed voices in the med lab. Anton jumped back and frantically poured over the readings coming from its sensors. Everything indicated cardiac arrest.

A couple of genorg troops glanced over in his direction as he stumbled away from the Lieutenant. Doc rocketed along his track toward the med tube and threw a warning bleat at Anton. He stepped further back and staggered over to the comm panel in sickbay.

He slapped haphazardly at the controls, "Rabbit to bridge, do you copy? Rabbit to bridge!"

Jacquie's voice came over the comm, "What's up Anton?"

He watched nervously as Doc cracked the med tube open and used three of its eight arms to remove the Lieutenant's body.

"Galena's gone into cardiac arrest. Doc's pulled her out of the tube." His eyes darted around as two of the genorg troops headed for the lift. "She's drawing a lot of attention from the soldiers. I'm, uh, going to see what I can do from here."

***

"Dammit!" cried Jacquie. "Derain can you stay on the bridge? I have got to keep this from getting out of hand."

A clamor erupted outside the Matilda as a leviathan collided with the vessel. Both Jacquie and Derain stumbled to keep their feet. They pressed their faces to the viewport with the hope that the behemoth turned away, but it kept pace with the Matilda.

A little shaken, Derain replied, "On it, Captain."

She wiped at her brow and keyed the comm to the engine room, "Barney? Luli? Can you meet me in sickbay? Things are about to go pear shaped."

She grabbed her pistol belt and blasted through the hatch on her way to the lift.

***

Luli turned off the comm and

confronted Barney, "You have anything in that box of yours that might be useful in this kind of situation?"

He gazed at her absentmindedly before his face lit up. He rummaged through a drawer and pulled out a small box and withdrew two spheres. He poked through another drawer until he removed a couple sets of earplugs. He tossed one pair to Luli and placed the other pair in his ears.

"Really?" she asked. "Stun grenades?"

He nodded in the affirmative as he tromped out into the main shaft. Luli followed him as he closed the hatch to the engine room and locked it shut. She gave him an inquiring look as if to ask why. He pointed to the grenades and then at the two hatches for the passenger containers. She gave a thumbs-up in understanding.

She floated down to the starboard hatch and he moved off to the port one. They both quietly locked the hatch plates and shot down to the hatch for the gym. Once they were through, Barney turned to lock that one as well.

"Is it going to be that bad?" she asked.

"If they're anywhere near as serious about eradicating the contaminated as they were planet side? I'm going to have to give a resounding yes." He fingered one of the grenades, "They aren't the joking type."

***

Anton kept track of the genorg soldiers from the corner of his eye while they gathered in the cargo bay. Everyone watched Doc as he outstretched an arm and sent an electrical impulse into the Lieutenant. Her body jerked under the defibrillator repeatedly without a recognizable change. To get a better look, Anton slid quietly over to the doors of the room when a shriek behind made him jump.

He whirled around in time to see Galena sitting upright on the table, her mouth wide open and eyes black as pitch. Doc's incision into her chest to gain access to her heart had become ragged from her sudden movement. Blood spattered out from the wound and the screech continued long after it should have.

A blunt object smacked against the back of Anton's head and he went down in a heap. Hands tugged at his holster. He tried to prevent them from taking his gun, but they kept batting his hands away.

Doc injected a fluid directly through the incision in Galena's chest. Her eyes cleared and the scream dwindled to silence. Someone stepped on the back of his hand and his wrist snapped. He yowled in pain as his pistol was yanked free of his grasp. His hand flopped loosely as it was pushed violently away.

A shot rang out. He watched in horrid fascination as a new hole blossomed in the

Lieutenant's chest. She slowly toppled off the operating table and spilled onto the floor like a broken doll. Another shot rang out and punctured Doc's plating. He thought he heard a third shot ring out from a distance, but wasn't sure as unconsciousness enfolded him.

***

Luli and Barney ran to the railing on the second deck when shots rang out from below. They threw a glance over the edge and caught a view of the wounded troops struggling with someone. Another shot rang out as Jacquie stepped out of the lift with her gun drawn, but pointed above the crowd.

Barney flashed a guilty look to Luli. She grimaced back at him. He yanked the pins on the two grenades and tossed them over the railing. They hunkered down as the grenades went off, back to back. The sonic waves from the explosions crashed into the walls of the hold and bounced back to the center of the cargo bay.

They waited a minute after the blasts cleared then took a peek over the railing. Genorgs were splayed out across the cargo bay decking in all directions. Luli looked toward the lift and nudged Barney in the ribs. He glanced over and spotted Jacquie lying on the decking, out cold.

He pulled out his ear plugs and waited until Luli had pulled hers out as well, "Well, she's going to be pissed."

seven

Wayfaring Stranger

Galena woke in a seated position surrounded by her sisters, but something was amiss. Their eyes, black as night, stared unblinkingly back at her. Confusion reigned within her as she stared back. Her vision shifted and she became lost in the crowd, staring back at herself. When her eyes widened, every set of eyes she could see did the same.

Suddenly, a great agony rushed into her and she cried out. She jerked upwards and found herself on top of an operating table surrounded by her sisters. Their rage and fear beat at her. Anton cried out as he was crushed into the decking under their feet. She doubled over from an impact to her chest and the sound of a shot echoed loudly in her ears. She gasped as the jerk of the impact threw her off the operating table. Her body slid to the decking and blessed unconsciousness engulfed her.

***

Jacquie groggily came to when the ship rocked as it was buffeted by the Major-knew-what from the outside. She struggled to focus on Derain and Barney as they trussed up the last of the soldiers in the cargo bay. The wall below the railing was blackened from a pair of small radius blasts and one of the sickbay doors looked like a spider had made itself a home within the cracked plas-glass. Jacquie slowly took into account her massive headache, the blast marks and then glared at Barney.

Barney felt the Captain's eyes burn a hole into the back of his head and he turned around sheepishly.

"Stun grenade?" She waited for the small nod, "Stun grenade. In a ship. On my ship! With me in the same room?" She dragged her body up into a standing position.

Luli's voice rang out from the sickbay, "Barney! Get in here! I'm losing her!"

Barney dropped what he had in his hands and ran past the fractured door. Jacquie forced her numb limbs forward and staggered after him. She threw a glance to Derain as he shoved one of the recently tied up troopers into a line against the bulkhead.

Jon Gray Lang

She asked, "Under control?"

"Under control," he replied as he dragged the last soldier over and propped her next to the previous one.

She swung back toward the med lab and spotted Luli crouched over the body of a genorg. The decking around it was slick with blood. Barney scrambled over to the supply cabinets and tore one of the doors open while Anton lay propped against a wall near the doors. He waved weakly in her direction before his bruised face centered back to Luli. Doc appeared to be offline and there was a new bullet hole in his chassis.

"What's going on, Lu?" she asked.

Luli grunted, "I'm keeping Galena from bleeding out right now! Put another sponge there, Barney. And put a clamp there, too!"

Jacquie struggled to get a glimpse of what the two of them were doing with the genorg on the floor. "What's up with Doc? Why isn't he operating?"

Barney glared over his shoulder, "Not now! Leave the questions for later!"

"I'll bring her up to speed," said Derain as he put his hand on Jacquie's arm. "Come over here and take a seat. You look pretty beat up yourself."

Derain kept her on her feet as she stumbled over to sit on a crate. He brushed a loose strand of hair from her face and placed it behind her ear. She feebly tried to knock his hand free.

Her hands dropped to her lap and she blinked a handful of times. Her expression sobered, "Bring me up to date."

"What's the last thing you remember?"

Her neck popped with the slight movement to keep Luli in her peripheral vision, "Anton called for help over the comm because the Lieutenant was going into cardiac arrest. I hopped on the lift and opened the doors to a mob scene down here. One of the genorg soldiers started shooting so I pulled my pistol and fired a round to distract them. Then there was an explosion and I woke up to find this." She gazed into his eyes, "That about covers it, frankly."

Derain uncrossed his arms and took a seat next to her on the crate.

Her eyes traveled back over to Anton, "Who's on the bridge right now?"

"No one at the moment." Derain set about examining the small nicks and cuts that decorated her skin from the grenades. Once he was satisfied that she was not going to die right then and there, he continued, "No need really. Matilda is heading toward one of those theoretical weak spots. We can't track where it is, so we can't rush it. Not much to do up there in the meantime."

He scraped at the dried blood trapped under his fingernails, "You didn't miss much, then. You've already figured out it was Barney that tossed a couple of stun grenades over the railing and

Jon Gray Lang

knocked everyone out cold. After the smoke cleared, they called me down to help with the cleanup."

"I can see all of that with my own eyes," she grumbled in exasperation. "What happened to Galena? And Anton, for that matter? Why is Doc offline?"

"From what we pieced together, Doc was in the middle of surgery on the Lieutenant when she woke up. As soon as the genorgs saw her blackened eyes, they went mad. During the ensuing scuffle with Rabbit, they broke his wrist, stole his gun, then shot her and Doc." He paused long enough to collect his thoughts, "We pulled the automaton offline."

"Why?"

"Anton said he saw it inject some sort of liquid into Galena during the surgery. Barney dug into his systems and found an incriminating log entry. The robot had been preprogrammed to do just that, if and when the opportunity arose. We took Doc offline until we have the time to check it for any other changes that might've been made. It seemed like the best plan."

He wrung his hands for a moment, "We ran some toxicology tests on the substance left in the needle housing and it matches that blue dust I found in Mr. Leon's belongings. It's a pretty sure bet that he or one of his people were involved."

She mulled this over as Luli worked hard to keep the newest member of her crew alive.

Derain got up and replaced Barney so that he could get started on a walled diagnostic for Doc. The Captain stared blankly in their general direction until Luli sat back and wiped a bloody streak across her brow. She threw Jacquie a nod to say that she was done followed by a shrug filled with uncertainty. Jacquie instinctively knew there were going to be more problems, but without more information, she wasn't sure what to do.

The comm lit up and that familiar genorg voice came over the line to echo solemnly in the cargo bay. "Captain? This is Delta 555-74K. We have affected our release from the locked containers. We are on our way to you." The pause that followed rang with dark promise, "Please reply, Captain."

The grumblings of the genorg troops in the cargo bay surrounded Jacquie and cleared the fog in her head. Once they were able to talk to Delta about the Lieutenant, mutiny was a sure bet. A full mutiny of close to four hundred trained soldiers against the five of them. She jerked upright and quickly jogged over to her crew.

"Is she stabilized? Can she be moved?"

"I just finished closing her up, Jacq," Luli responded tiredly.

"We need to get her top side as soon as possible. That includes us, too." She spun and faced Derain, "Grab any medical supplies that she might need and get her into the lift. The hold is

Jon Gray Lang

about to be overrun by a ton of angry, armed soldiers wanting her blood."

"And ours," muttered Rabbit.

eight

Army of Me

Soldier Delta floated next to the hatch in the main shaft while one of her soldiers cut through the locking bolt. There was a brief burst of light before Delta kicked open the door and slipped out to land on the decking in the gym.

Her platoon filed out past her. Some went into the machine room while others moved up to the hatch at the other end of the gym. Within a minute, she received the affirmative all clear for both rooms.

She turned back to the main shaft, "Gamma? Please secure the engine room."

"Sir, yes sir," saluted Gamma. She moved down to the squad at work on the lock of the other passenger carrier. Once the hatch popped open, she pointed to the trooper with the cutter,

"Rho-11, get the engine room opened."

The lock to the gym was summarily burned through. Delta stepped through the hatch into the cargo bay and up to the railing. She looked down into the open bay and observed her sister soldiers as they released the few who were still bound. She shouted down to the one in charge, "Omega, how do we fare?"

Omega waved two soldiers to the lift doors before she responded, "Cargo bay and sickbay secure. No fatalities. Two of the ship's crew are wounded and they took to the upper decks." She stopped to listen as one of her troops whispered in her ear, "One of the wounded showed signs of contagion. She took a round to the chest. The other wounded is the one called Rabbit."

Delta called back down, "Do we have the identity of the infected?"

"Yes, sir. It was the First Soldier."

***

Communications Officer Shimada Mariko approached Captain Kaplean on the bridge. She waited at a respectful distance while he brought his conversation with Mr. Cordelan to a close.

After the scanner technician moved back to his station, the Captain caught sight of her. Her bright eyes sparkled with the promise of hope. "I hope you have good news for me, Ms. Shimada. In truth, we are at a standstill in this investigation."

Jon Gray Lang

Her fingers flew across her data pad, "We ran searches with the specifics that you received from the Remus, and the results were mostly fruitless..."

"I was hoping for good news, Ms. Shimada," he interrupted.

Flustered, Mariko regathered herself, "Of course. My apologies, sir. We cross-referenced open warrants for the Vogelgesang survivors against the bounty hunters who had tagged those warrants. We discovered an old warrant for Dr. Saric which had been denied due to his untimely demise. The denied warrant was under the docket of a bounty hunter named Derain Tiwi." A satisfied smile settled across her lips, "Derain Tiwi closely matches the physical description for the bounty hunter we have on file. His records point to Aketi being his home world."

"We were also able to pull a copy of his holo ID." She pulled up the image on her data pad and presented it to him.

The description he had received from Captain Ellsbeth didn't do the man justice. A face carved from granite with the eyes of a killer stared back at him, but it was a match.

The smile he gave to Mariko was warm, "Excellent work, Ms. Shimada. Excellent work. Would you please inform Dr. Wyeth that we are underway?"

"Of course, sir." She saluted as she returned to her station.

Jon Gray Lang

The Captain addressed his navigation officer, "Ms. Grissom, please set our heading for the Aken system."

"Our course heading is set, Captain."

***

The latest demand from Delta faded out over the ship's comm. The soldiers had been fast. The crew of the Matilda had barely cleared the cargo bay before the genorgs had taken control of the first two decks.

Once they had gotten Galena situated on the large table in the lounge, Barney had gone back to lock down the lift at the third deck as a preventative measure. The lift doors on the top deck had been sealed as well, but no one expected them to hold for very long. The hopes on both measures slowing the soldiers down for any length of time were low. Barney could faintly hear the cutter at work on the lift's flooring even before he headed back.

Barney walked with a heavy heart. The ultimatum they had been given required an answer and soon. The others had chosen him to force a decision from the Captain. Luckily, she hadn't gone too far. He found her seated with her back against a bulkhead near the airlock. An open bottle of whiskey rested between her knees.

"Want a slug?" she asked after she took a long swig. "To be honest, this is the only thing that makes any sense to me, right now."

Barney's forehead furrowed as he looked carefully at the label on the bottle, "Is that...?"

"It sure is," she patted the decking next to her. "The very last bottle from when my parents were murdered, you were taken and the whole of my life changed forever." She took another pull from the bottle before she held it in her hands and stared into the amber liquid. "I was saving this one for the best day the future had in store for me. The very best day. Ha!"

Barney slid down next to her. He took the bottle from her hands and took a sip.

"But why save it for the best day when the second-worst day I could have would be perfect!" She tilted her head to the side and gazed into his downcast eyes, "I miss my folks, Barney. I miss them more every single day."

"I know lass. I miss them too." A grunt escaped him as he located the cork on the decking and placed it back in the neck, "But we don't have time for this right now, we need a decision."

"Terrible decisions are voted on by everyone, that's the ship's rule," she groused. "Has everyone voted? Did you vote?"

"I'm holding mine until..." Barney stopped mid-sentence as crashing sounds and yells emanated from the lounge. He shot a glance down the hall and then stared back at her. He carefully set the bottle down and headed off to the lounge with purpose growing in every stride.

***

Gamma's voice echoed up the shaft, "No go on the lift controls, Delta. Controls were cut to the lower decks."

Delta shouted back down, "Understood. Prep the cutter." She nudged the soldier above her, "Go ahead and strap in Rho-11. We'll need to burn through the base of the lift."

The gas torch made its way up the chain of soldiers on the ladder that ran the length of the shaft. Both genorgs strapped themselves down. Delta handed the nozzle up to Rho-11 and then worked to hold her steady in the lack of gravity.

As Rho-11 set the cutter to the base of the lift, she murmured, "I don't think I've ever used the cutter this much before."

Delta grimaced, "Strange times, these."

It was slow work, but a small hole beaded in glowing metal was shaping up nicely. The torch cut off and the handle was passed down to Delta. She passed it down to the trooper below her while Rho-11 pushed upward. There was a sharp 'tink' sound and then a thud. Delta looked up as Rho-11 disappeared into the hole.

Moments later her face reappeared, "All clear, sir."

Delta called out, "Everyone, down.

And stow that torch! Move, move, move!"

***

Jacquie gazed at the bottle with longing, but got to her feet and followed the engineer. She couldn't figure out how the genorg soldiers could have gotten into the lounge so quickly. She loosened her pistol in its holster.

When she entered the lounge, she stopped in bewilderment. Galena held Luli above her head. The Lieutenant's eyes were wide open, but her face was devoid of emotion. Without any effort, she threw the cyborg into the galley. Derain skipped back and pulled his pistol from his holster.

"No!" Luli cried out as she disentangled herself from the pots and pans.

Galena's head twisted around to where Derain stood. He fired a shot and she moved fractionally. While the movement was tiny, it was incredibly fast. The round passed over her shoulder and smacked into the wall behind her. Without stopping, she bolted straight toward him.

The burst of speed she achieved was bizarre to behold. Her movements were stiff, almost mechanical. She chopped him in the wrist and pulled the slide of his pistol completely off. He tried to backpedal out of the way, but his movements were too slow and he realized there was no escape.

Somehow she knew, even with

Jon Gray Lang

unfocused eyes, that Barney was coming for her. She rolled her hand along Derain's jawline. As he spun, she forced him directly into Barney's path and they went down in a tangle of arms and legs. Jacquie yanked her pistol free. Before she could even aim, the gun was knocked out of her grasp. It crashed against the decking and slid into a corner.

A hand wrapped around Jacquie's throat and lifted her off the floor. She stared into Galena's eyes, but there was no one there, just a dead blank stare. She watched in horror as Galena's movements segued from its mechanical rigidness to an amorphous fluidity. Her demeanor changed and her head tilted strangely to the side. Jacquie couldn't look away as inky lines streaked out from the pupils of the genorg's eyes. She watched in horrid fascination even as her breathing became labored.

With a sudden movement, Galena slipped forward and sniffed her face, then the hollow of her neck. She pulled back and those midnight eyes reflected Jacquie's struggle for breath.

Her mouth twisted into a dark smile and her words undulated through the room in the abrupt silence, "You smell like an enemy tastes..."

***

Hacking the lift controls from the inside had been a simple job. With a quick slap to the back of the hacker, Delta rode up in the lift with the first set of troops. And it was filled to maximum capacity.

They pried the doors open and the sounds of screams mixed with fighting echoed down the hallway. She checked her rifle and watched in satisfaction as the soldiers in the lift did the same. She sucked in a breath and moved out into the hallway on the top deck. The noise ahead cut off like a switch had been thrown.

"Send the lift back down for the next load. The rest of you, follow me." She waved her soldiers forward and they double-timed it down the hall toward the lounge.

Once her people entered the room, Delta tracked the position of the crew members. The cyborg pilot stood in a pile of cookware far back to the left. The small engineer and the tall bounty hunter lay on the floor next to each other near the room entrance. In the middle of the lounge sat the Captain. She clutched the First Soldier in her lap.

Delta pointed at two of her soldiers, "You and you, cover them. You two, cover the cyborg." She walked slowly toward the Captain and kept her rifle aimed at the Lieutenant.

***

Shock colored Jacquie's expression when she looked down into the Lieutenant's face. A voice spoke sharply and she looked up. She watched numbly as the genorg troopers slowly moved in and held her crew at gunpoint. Her gaze settled on the genorg commander. Delta slowly walked toward her while the barrel of her rifle pointed unwaveringly at the Lieutenant.

Galena jerked, twisted her head and stared up at Jacquie. The clarity of her bright green eyes was apparent. Tears streaked down her face and joined the blood that soaked through her medical gown.

She whimpered, "What is happening to me?"

nine

Tracks of My Tears

Mr. Leon kept an eye out the window of his office as the Copperhead launched from the nearby space port on Mithuna. After the ship broke atmosphere, he headed back to his desk. With a keystroke, he released the funds for a donation. It should arrive at its final destination within the week, though he might not get a response for a month.

But it was of little import. A contingent plan to strike fear into those who might not accept his currency was already in place. An odd smile graced his lips, "To coin a phrase, my arms are quite long and my fingers are dipped into so many pies." A lead on who ordered that pursuit ship and why would be found eventually.

He had only arrived at this office yesterday, but his people had already become quite

Jon Gray Lang

motivated by his presence. It had been many years since one of his brood had been stationed in this system and he was glad to find nothing amiss.

His employees had been surprised when he had requested a copy of the building's floor plan. Their shock hadn't been alleviated when he said it was a search for any unknown entrances. The search hadn't revealed anything due to the newness of the building, but it had set rumors spinning.

Mr. Leon took a sip from the small teacup on his desk. The crew of the Matilda still occupied his mind. There had been no word of the ship since the ordnance delivery and, in this case, no news was not necessarily good news. The crew of that freighter was in possession of one of his greatest secrets and knowledge was dangerous, depending on where it fell.

Besides, he detested loose ends.

***

The vessel, designation M33, slipped through the jump gate into the Aken system. The gate crew sent an identification request. Once they received the Special Ops passcode, that comm channel closed quickly. The frequency remained dark, but the local fleet ships maneuvered out from their course.

"We are en route to Aketi, sir. Our arrival time is within 23 hours."

"Thank you, Ms. Grissom," Captain

Kaplean replied.

Dr. Wyeth had been perturbed with the lack of leads for the hunt of her genorg creation. Even though the Doctor had been present when the target ship had disappeared off Ninguiz, she still wanted and expected results immediately. The woman was difficult to work with at the best of times, but her patience had worn to a thin veneer on this voyage.

Captain Kaplean asked, "Ms. Shimada? Please, tight beam the local Consortium representative on Aketi. Have the Tiwi family detained for questioning. I would like them to be available to me within a solar day."

"The message has been sent, Captain."

ten

Full Moon

Delta sighted down her rifle to the revered First Soldier and watched as tears ran down her face. The green of her eyes, so like mine she thought, shone brightly in the ambient light of the lounge. She moved her finger away from the trigger and stared deeply into those crystal clear eyes. Her weapon came to a rest on her shoulder.

The Lieutenant's mannerisms spoke volumes to the genorgs. A look of peace etched itself across her countenance, followed quickly by that same look appearing on the soldier's faces. The genorg troops all waited as Galena nodded in acquiescence toward their commander. Her eyes closed in acceptance and she waited for the impact of the killing shot.

Jacquie, her eyes reddened with the

tears she refused to let loose, held tightly to Galena. She was cornered, with no way out. Memories of the moment when her parents were held at gunpoint surfaced to her mind. Trapped in that moment when there was nothing she could do except die with them. She had always known that had been the only other real option. But fear had taken her and she had chosen to hide.

She shook herself furiously. *'You made a choice! You may be damned for it, but you chose your fate. And you will continue to make choices, be they good or bad, until there are none left for you to make. So no more hiding, no more fears,* she admonished herself. *No more!'*

The Matilda rocked hard to port and swung wildly to starboard. Delta lost her balance in the sudden shifting of the ship. Jacquie shoved Galena to the side and leapt forward to rip the rifle out of Delta's hands. She slammed the rifle butt into the genorg's face which sent her tumbling to the decking from the impact. Other genorg soldiers lost their footing as the ship continued to rock. Once they had recovered their balance, they found the Captain of this small vessel facing them. Her legs were locked out for stormy seas and a rifle lay in her hands, held at chest level.

"No more. Do you hear me! No more," she growled. The ship tilted forward then rolled to the aft. Jacquie stood there unaffected by the turbulence. She had lived her entire life on this ship and knew how to hold her stance no matter how rough the journey. "If anyone fires a shot, I will kill every last one of you. I will open this ship to the nightmares out there and none of us will survive. Do you hear me? None of us..." She strode forward and kicked Delta in the stomach, "Is that understood?"

Delta lay prone on the decking across from the Lieutenant. She stared into those bright green eyes. "So clear," a part of her brain muttered to her. "So clear." Delta felt the pain of the blow but ignored it. She whispered into the open air, "What makes you distinct? What separates you from us; that keeps you unchanged?"

She rolled onto her back and stared up at the woman who held off her soldiers all by her lonesome. Her brow wrinkled in confusion, "How did you create so much conviction in one of them? So different..."

***

Luli had remained motionless in the back of the galley during Jacquie's outburst. It was only as the troops laid down their arms and stepped back that she began to relax. Something caught the corner of her eye; stars twinkled in the distance. She did a double-take and stared out the viewport and it was filled with stars!

"Stars?" she murmured tentatively until it finally sank in.

Barney perked up and followed her eyes to the viewport. "Stars?"

Jon Gray Lang

"Stars!" she cried out loud. "Jacq! There are stars! Stars out there! I think we're free! I think we..."

"...fell through!" Barney and Luli shouted in unison.

"Go make sure, Lu," Jacquie ordered.

As Luli ran past everyone on her way to the bridge, Derain stepped forward and collected the weapons the soldiers had surrendered. Barney got up to help him but suddenly backed up away from the hatch.

Followed closely by Gamma, Anton scratched at his side and stumbled into the room. He yawned briefly and stretched his good arm as he looked around, "Did I miss something?"

eleven

Way Out There

"I was right!" Luli cried out. "We're back! Back in our own space!" She tracked the stars through the bow port, then rechecked the nav system, "But, I have absolutely no idea where here is."

Jacquie strode onto the bridge, followed closely by Derain and Anton. Sandwiched between them were the three genorg leaders. Derain's pistol stayed locked onto the soldiers as Anton had them stand against the bulkhead.

Jacquie brushed her hair back as she slumped into the pilot's seat, "Barney's taking Galena back down to sickbay. What can you tell me, Lu?"

"The Matilda definitely tumbled through a soft spot, but I don't recognize the system." Luli stared into the pilot's visor, "It's got a K-class star with seven planets in its gravitational embrace. The fourth one out should be habitable, but I'm not getting any electronic traffic. To be honest, I don't even know if we're still in Consortium controlled space."

"Well, keep digging."

Luli jacked into the nav system, "I am on the job, mon Capitan! I'll pull all my old charts and cross my digits on the hopes of a match."

Captain Delahaye spun her chair and glared at the three genorgs, "Can I trust you and your people to keep the peace?"

"We do not consider Lieutenant Chadov a threat. We are at your command, Captain," responded Delta.

"Glad to hear it," Jacquie replied. "Go find my engineer and see what your sisters can help with. I'll meet up with the lot of you later so we can continue to discuss your futures, alright? Derain? Anton? Let them pass."

Derain grumbled as he slid his pistol home, "You think that's wise, Jacq? They could wipe us out in a minute."

"Exactly. They could wipe us out, but they didn't." She scowled at him, "You have any better ideas?"

He stepped back from the fierceness of her response, "Well, no I don't but..."

"Good. I need you and Anton to check out that fourth planet. I need to know where the hell we are." She continued to glower at him, "The sooner, the better."

"Of... of course, Captain." Derain stomped through the hatch, "Come on Rabbit. We've got to get the Waratah prepped."

"Wow. She tore you a new one in there." Anton prodded.

"Shut up, Anton."

***

Anton struggled to pull on his spacesuit as he strolled into the sickbay. He made his way toward Barney, who hummed quietly to himself, while he finished replacing the Lieutenant's torn stitches. Anton gripped him by the shoulder as the Titan put a patch of plasflesh on the wound.

Barney jumped back in shock, "What in the seven hells, man?"

"Oh, sorry. I didn't mean to startle you," Anton said sheepishly.

Barney growled, "Well if you had been awake for the past few hours you'd understand how unsettling it is to have someone sneaking around!"

"Everyone's so on edge now," Anton grumbled as Barney headed toward the blood chemistry analyzer. "A person can't even walk around without people getting bloody jumpy."

A loud sigh exploded from Anton as he followed him. "I should be leaving now but I just need to know... is she going to make it?"

"Oh, she'll live. As long as she doesn't rip out her stitches again... or get shot or a million other things." Barney saw the concern mirrored in Anton's eyes, "Don't worry, Luli did good work. She'll be up and about in a few days, no worse for wear."

A loud ding rang from the analyzer. Barney flipped through the reports and his forehead wrinkled in surprise, "Huh. Her blood work is clear. Hopefully, her behavior was just a side effect..."

Barney realized he was talking to himself. Anton now stood next to the Lieutenant's med tube.

"I'll, uh, leave you two alone."

Anton gave him a halfhearted wave before he turned back and gazed at Galena. She looked so peaceful; all the worries had cleared from her face. He reached in and gave her hand a squeeze, "Barney says you'll be up and running in a few days. Could you do me an extra and take it easy until I get back?"

A light smile flickered across her lips before it disappeared again. He smiled in response.

It changed to a grimace as Derain's voice came through the comm, "Rabbit, are you coming or not? We have to go!"

"On my way Derain... on my way..."

***

Jon Gray Lang

"You lot right chewed up my boat," Barney grunted at the assembled genorg troopers. "Which one of you cut my hatches?" He peered down the line until one of them stepped forward. "So you're the one, eh?"

"Yes sir, Mr. de Lagnel," replied Rho-11.

He came to a stop in front of her and put his hands on his hips, "The rules on this ship are simple. You break it, you fix it. So choose your team and repair my hatches. You don't know where something is or can't find it, come find me. Got it?"

"Sir, yes sir!" Rho-11 saluted in earnest. She glanced up and down the line and called out to a dozen troopers. The sound of their footsteps receded as they ran toward the main shaft.

Barney paced back and forth for a few minutes before he cleared his throat. "As I'm sure most of you know, we're off the beaten track. Now, I have a plan to send probes out into this system with the hopes of rectifying that. Who amongst you has received some technical or mechanical training?" At the random show of hands, he continued, "I'm going to need about twenty of you for this. Follow me up to the workshop on the second deck. The rest of you can go about your business."

twelve

Black Sun

Jacquie gazed out the bow port and felt at peace. The sky was littered with the bright pinpricks of stars. The edge of a moon was limned with the sunlight from this system. It hadn't been a dream. They hadn't been thrown back amongst the monsters.

The week of travel had been slow but it had been productive. According to Barney, repairs were coming along nicely. The Matilda would have functioning hatches and a lift with a floor soon.

The question as to what system they were in still remained unanswered. Luli had scoured her star charts and been unable to find a match. The probes weren't assembled yet. On top of that, they still hadn't received a response from the Waratah.

Jon Gray Lang

The comm chirped before the Lieutenant's voice came over, "Captain? Are you there?"

Jacquie flipped the bridge comm on, "Morning Galena, or evening I suppose. It's been hard to keep track lately. How are you feeling?"

"Oh me? Besides some inflammation around my stitches, I remain in working order," Galena answered. "Could I ask a boon of you and Luli in the cargo bay? I... I need some assistance and you are the only ones I know of that can help."

"Sure, Lieutenant. We can be down in a few." Jacquie threw an arched eyebrow at Luli, "Should we be concerned?"

Relief flooded through the comm, "Thank you. I've been working with my sisters down here and their naivety scares me."

"If they're anything like you, I can see why you'd be concerned," Jacquie joked.

Galena ignored the remark, "Anyway, I've been teaching them tricks and tactics that I've picked up in my time abroad. My hope is that it will help prepare them for the unexpected. They've been absorbing it rapidly."

Luli asked, "So what can we help you with?"

There was a long stretch of dead air before Galena's voice took on the quality of a whisper, "I've been trying to teach them that dancing activity you showed me, but I'm having trouble explaining what it's for."

Jacquie glanced over at Luli and started laughing. Luli tried to keep it in, but the laughter erupted from her as well. Unfortunately, they had left the comm channel wide open.

"I really don't think this is a laughing matter," Galena said indignantly. The peals of laughter grew louder over the open comm.

Jacquie struggled to control her outburst, "We're on our way down, Lieutenant. See you in a few." She clicked the comm off.

"Alright Jacq, let's get this dance class a swayin'!" Luli hopped out of her seat and sprinted to the lift.

"So much energy. Maybe I'll just sit back and watch while you teach," Jacquie giggled as she followed her into the lift.

"Ha! You need a break away from those charts and supply listings," Luli chortled. "You know you want to make them dance." She grabbed the Captain's hand and forced her into a pirouette, "You need to make them dance."

Jacquie grabbed Luli by the hip and led her into a dip, "Hey! Looks like Barney got that hole patched in here!"

The lift doors parted and Luli straightened up. She brushed her hair back before Jacquie pushed her out. A snort escaped the pilot when Jacquie punched her in the shoulder. Their smiles wilted when faced with the somber looks from the genorgs who stood at attention in the cargo bay.

Jon Gray Lang

"Captain?"

"There you are, Galena. What have you covered so far?" asked Jacquie.

Galena stepped out from the crowd. "I've only covered a few beginning moves."

Luli squinted around the cargo bay, "I don't hear anything. What have you been using for music?"

"I, uh, haven't gotten into music yet."

"What?" Luli cried out. "Well, there's your problem right there. How do you expect anyone to move to the music if there isn't any music to move to?"

Galena piqued at the statement. "Music is such a heady subject. I thought I would start with movement first."

"Heady, schmeady! The whole point behind dancing is music!" Luli admonished.

Jacquie's laughter rang out in the quiet cargo bay. "I'll go turn something on."

Luli spied a raised hand in the middle of the crowd. "Who's got their hand up? Come on, step out and ask your question."

A genorg soldier made her way to the front of the crowd. As she opened her mouth to ask the question, Luli interrupted her, "And you are?"

"Oh. I am designated Alpha-17."

Music with a solid thumping beat began to play over the comm system. A smile cracked across Luli's face as the genorgs searched for the origination of the sound. She nodded in sync with the rhythm. "Nice to meet you, Alpha-17. What's your question?"

"What is the purpose of this dancing? What is the point to all of this?"

Luli crossed her arms and put a finger to her chin. Jacquie snickered as she joined the pilot in front of the assembled troops. "Come on, old lady! Answer the young woman's question. "What's all this for?"

"What is this all for?" Luli pondered loudly. "I can only tell you what it is for me. Old Captain Grumpy Pants here can tell you hers, too."

"Captain Grumpy Pants?" quipped Jacquie.

Luli's head tilted and the grin on her face grew. "Music and dance keep me alive; they've kept me going for centuries. They get me through the bad days and make the good days all the better."

Galena answered, "It's the human thing to do?"

"Exactly," replied Jacquie. "It's the human thing to do. It doesn't matter if you're a cyborg, a natural-born or a genorg. It brings you closer to your humanness."

Luli followed with, "And isn't that all we are trying to achieve with our time in this universe? To be as human as we can be?"

A confusion of chatter flowed out from the lines of genorgs. The skin around Luli's eyes crinkled from her huge grin. It was mirrored in

Jacquie's face as she patted her on the back. Galena's face also broke out into a huge smile as the chatter died down.

Alpha-17 turned back to face the three women. "Ms. Qing, would you teach us to be more human?"

"Will I ever? Space is going to be tight in here, so we're going to do this in groups. Form up into three lines."

Luli moved to the front of the middle line and twirled to face the lift. Jacquie took the line to the left and Galena the line to the right. Luli nodded to the two women. She grabbed the hands of the genorg who stood behind her and placed them on her hips.

"Hands on the hips of the lady in front of you. Now, follow her movements and listen to how it fits with the beat of the music." Luli swung her right hip out and then her left hip.

By the third song, the entire room swayed to the beat. Laughter and giggles percolated up from the hard-as-nails troopers as each of them began to flow into the movements.

Luli glanced behind her and shouted out, "Now it's time to add some steps!" She threw her right leg forward and then brought it back. She then repeated the action with her left leg. Her grin grew infectious. Suddenly, she called out, "You keep doing this well, we can move on up to the Hokey Pokey!"

Alpha-17 muttered to the soldier in

front of her, "Being human is weird."

***

Barney stood just outside the hangar as he kept an eye on his team of probe builders. They had modified an old shoulder launch mechanism that had come onboard from Ninguiz to launch the probes. The probes themselves were simply sections of pipe that had a small engine in the back and a sensor array located in the tip. He gave his final instructions to the ladies and watched as they clomped off as a group to the airlock.

He turned to find Galena standing silently next to him. He jumped back in shock and barely caught the slight, but amused, smile that crossed her lips before it segued back to its stoic expression.

Anton had mentioned that her differences to the other genorgs had become more pronounced. And now having so many to compare her to, he had to agree. It was something about the way she held herself, but it was also something in her eyes. She had seen and done too much in her life to not be changed by it. Those moments were etched into her being and stood her in stark contrast from her sisters.

"Well?" he asked. "What can I do for you, lass?"

"Everyone has been so busy of late that I haven't had the chance to ask a favor of you.

I need you to show me how to repair Doc." Her hands opened and grasped at the open air, "He's still offline."

"He's offline for a reason..."

She replied, "Well, we need him online. There are too many patients for Luli to handle on her own."

"He's offline because someone altered his programming," grunted Barney. "The only reason we even know that is because of what happened to you."

She quietly stared at him for a moment before she walked off toward the lift. When she stopped at the corner, she looked back at him, "Well? Are you coming?"

He looked at her quizzically, "What?"

"You once told me that if I was responsible for Doc getting damaged, that you would make me fix him." She put her hands on her hips, "It looks like I am responsible. Here I stand, ready to do my duty as you said I must. Besides, the ship's repairs are almost done and it looks like your probes are built and being launched. So, are you coming or not?"

He gazed into her eyes and determination stared back. A smile quirked his lips as he rolled his eyes, "Right behind you."

***

The sickbay was as quiet as a morgue.

Most of the patients had been moved out except for those few that were still in their med tubes. The only sound was the low, constant rumble of the ship.

Barney flicked the overhead lights on and the two of them physically inspected the robotic surgeon. His torso hung from the ceiling like a giant broken toy and the lights on his chassis remained dark.

Barney glanced at Galena and pointed to the bullet hole, "I'll need you to pull that plate off and check for any internal damage that might've been done. I'll also need you to disassemble the needle injector and its fluid reservoirs over there." She followed his pointing finger to the injector assembly. "Might as well get to it, but, uh, mind your stitches, would you? I don't have the steadiest hands for surgery... on people."

She admonished, "Except for Luli, I can't think of anyone else on board this boat with steadier ones."

"Shush, you," he rebuked. He squatted next to the undercarriage of the medical robot. "I'm going to strip the brain housing down and see what I can find."

The two of them worked in mutual silence until Galena pried loose the plate pierced by the bullet. The round had crashed into a circuit board and shattered it within the housing. Nicks and cuts in the chamber showed where the fragments had hit before coming to a rest.

She called down to Barney, "What

kind of weapon was used in this? This isn't a standard-issue round."

Barney's voice rolled up to her, "Think it was Anton's. You'd have to ask him about it."

"Hmm." She flicked out remnants of the projectile, "Do you have any small hydraulic hose on hand?"

"Check in the cabinet over there," he replied.

As she rummaged through the cabinet, he asked her, "How are you doing, anyway?" The housing plate came off in his hands and he set it to the side with a dull clang. "Well, everything looks alright in here."

"Me? I'm still functional. I think this'll do." She wandered back over to the automaton, "I guess I feel different, but I can't explain it to you in a way that makes sense." She set the new parts down and swept out the broken bits that littered the compartment, "I look at my sisters and I feel separate... Like I am no longer one of them. But I know that I am." She turned toward him, "Does that make sense?"

He was quiet as he gave thought to her words, "Probably not in exactly the way you mean it, but I think I understand."

She pulled the mangled tubing out and snipped a new piece to fit. The ruined circuit board came out next and she wandered back over to the cabinet and looked for a replacement. "Is this a common feeling for humans?"

"For us natural-borns, it can be. We can be part of a larger group and still feel disconnected from it." He spied a data drive jammed into one of the old ports. He exclaimed as he pulled it out, "Aha! Think today might be my lucky day. How bad was the damage in there?"

"Nothing serious. A hose was cut, but I've already replaced it. One of the boards was destroyed but I'm popping a new one in right now. Besides that, just some scratches." She screwed the housing plate back on and shifted over to the injector assembly.

"You see anything out of place in the injector housing?" he asked.

"Nothing yet, but I just got the module removed." She took it over to an open section of counter and pulled up a stool.

He searched around a little bit before he got up and connected his data pad to Doc. "I'm going to run another isolated diagnostic while you break that down, alright?"

"Got it, Mr. de Lagnel," she said offhandedly as she threw a salute.

He brought the automaton's system up and cut the access to its chassis. "Doc, I need you to run a report on any changes made to you within the past couple months. Someone tampered with your brain."

A tinny version of Doc's voice emanated from Barney's data pad, "Chu ta de? Ee chu ta de?"

"Yes, you were. That's why I'm asking you to run it! Just do it!" he cried.

A lilting laugh escaped from Galena as she pulled the fluid cartridge cylinder free from its casing. She went to inventory the multiple liquids within it and one of the canisters didn't match the existing registry. Curiosity struck her as she popped the container out and poured its contents onto the counter.

Barney glanced over and caught her pouring out some of the blue dust and yelled, "Don't touch that!"

She jerked at his voice and spilled some onto the back of her hand. It was quickly absorbed through her epidermal layer. A small squeak escaped her and the cartridge fell from her nerveless fingers. As she slumped out of her seat, her head smacked against the corner of the table.

"Galena!" Barney dropped everything and ran over to her, "Galena, are you alright? Galena! Answer me!"

But she didn't move. He picked her up and lifted her onto the operating table. Her pulse had definitely slowed down. He prodded her, but she remained unresponsive. He tore his eyes away and stared at where his data pad hung out of Doc's chassis. He cursed to himself before he reconnected Doc to his body.

"Figure out what's wrong with her now! Don't even try to say or do anything else!" he shouted.

thirteen

Insane in the Brain

Derain brought the Waratah into the hangar and eased her down to the decking. Once the mag-locks cycled, Anton reached over and triggered the hangar doors, then the hatch to the ship. Both men unstrapped themselves and walked out into the open bay.

The mood in the airlock changing room was a somber one. Their eyes slid away from each other as they stripped out of their spacesuits. Derain left the room first, followed shortly by Anton. On their way to the lift, voices rang out from the bridge.

At the bridge hatch, Jacquie clicked the comm off and her fingers pinched the bridge of her nose. Derain stepped in first and gave her shoulder a light squeeze. Anton hung back and watched the two of them. There was a level of familiarity there that he hadn't noticed before. A pang of guilt hit him hard in the stomach but he didn't let it show.

"What's wrong, Jacq? Who was that?" Anton asked in a rush.

She dropped her hand and her hardened eyes peered back at him, "It was Barney. Galena has collapsed and she's not responding. On top of that, Doc is still out of commission." She looked away, "For what it's worth, Luli's already on her way down."

Anton shifted against the wall, "I'll see if they need any help."

The Captain's shoulders bowed after Anton disappeared around the corner. The silence on the bridge was thick. Derain stood there, uncertain of what to do or say.

Jacquie waved him to a seat, "Please sit. Let me know what you found. We could use some good news right about now."

"I don't have any good news," he grimaced. "That planet is dead. It used to be inhabited, but it's nothing but a graveyard now. Ruined cities dot the surface. We didn't even get a peep on any of the band waves. At a guess, I'd say war broke out and there were no winners."

"Did anything look recognizable?" she asked. "Anything that might give us a clue as to what system this is? Or where we are?"

"Not that we could tell," he replied.

"Human settlement? Sure. But who and where?
No idea."

"So we still don't know where in the
Gods-be-damned galaxy we are. Without a
reference point, we don't know which way to go."
Jacquie's voice snapped, "Our problems keep
mounting. Supplies are running low because we
have a hold full of hungry mouths. I don't know
what to do with them and they don't have a clue,
either. To make matters worse, there is something
wrong with Galena but we don't know what it is or
how to fix it. Or even if she can be saved."

Derain shook his head, "I don't have
any answers for you."

Jacquie punched the armrest, "Hooray
for a lose-lose situation then."

***

The lift rumbled its way down to the
first deck and the impatient trudge of Anton's boots
rebounded from the walls. Once the elevator came
to a stop, he squeezed out past the doors as they
opened. He nearly tripped over one of the soldiers
camped in the cargo bay in his hurry to get to the
med lab. It almost didn't register to him that the
genorgs were on their knees in concentric half-
circles that radiated outward from the operating
table. He stopped for a moment and shook his
head, "Huh."

He could just make out Luli jacked

into Doc's chassis while Barney pounded away at his data pad on the floor. Galena, who was paler than usual, lay motionless on the operating table.

The doors swished closed behind him as he headed over to check on her, "How is she? Is she alive? Stable?"

"Anton, glad to see you back," grunted Barney.

"Alive?" Luli grouched, "Yes. Stable? Mostly. How is she? We don't know." A grimace played briefly across her face as she pulled the jack out from behind her ear, "I hope Doc is cleared soon. I don't know how much storage space I'll have left with all these medical processes rummaging around in here," she tapped at her skull. "Anton, it is good to see you back."

He bent down and gave her a hug, "Is there anything we can do for her?"

"Not without knowing more about what she's going through," Barney muttered. "As for Doc, I think it might be safe to reconnect him to his chassis. But I still want him cut off from the ship's systems. I've come across a string of errors between the two since Doc went nuts."

"So I can dump all this data...?" asked Luli.

Barney stopped her, "Keep it for now." He twirled the data drive in his hand, "I need to know what's on this thing before we make any final decisions about our automated friend."

Jon Gray Lang

***

Tunnels... Hallways... No beginnings and no ends in sight... Endless... Like swimming, the thought bubbled to the surface of her mind. But who am I? Where am I?

Galena slowly came to herself, but still, she felt lost, disconnected from everything. It was dark with a tinge of redness as if her eyes were clenched tight against a bright star. She forced her lids apart, but the darkness still enveloped her, buoyed her. Nothing felt familiar except the sensation of weightlessness. The sort of weightlessness one experiences when suspended in a liquid. She hesitantly stretched out all her limbs and nothing came into contact with her.

The hairs on the back of her neck tingled as she sensed that she was being watched. The mental pressure of whatever observed her grew until it blew across her mind in undulating waves. Small points of light flickered in the distance as the presence of that which surrounded her grew closer. The pressure tightened around her. The bellow of a giant beast crashed into her and sent her tumbling. The points of light grew larger until they resolved into eyes. Eyes, green like hers, from many faces. But fear radiated outward from them. Galena spun around and they lay in all directions.

"Hello?" she said hesitantly into the darkness, and the darkness filled her mouth. But she did not choke on that which she floated in.

Jon Gray Lang

Another bellow hit her and deep vibrations pummeled her bones. Round and round she tumbled until the rippling wave of sound slowly petered out. In shock, she lay still as the presence seemed to lose interest in her. The darkness slowly faded into a hazy dimness until she was able to make out some details.

Around her in all directions kneeled her sisters, but each one was disfigured, fractured. Another trumpeting blast enveloped her. Her body slammed against a bulkhead before she collapsed to the decking of a ship. With a shudder, she looked around and the hallway was filled with her sisters; their eyes, the color of night, bored into her own. Voices echoed in her head. Her own voice echoed back. Who am I? Where am I? Over and over the words repeated until it was a deafening cacophony.

She clenched her eyes shut and clapped her hands over her ears until the voices faded away. Wetness trickled down her back and she reached a hand to it. Her fingers came back bloodied. A cut in her back oozed slowly. Her eyes traveled up and spied a bent sign that hung loosely on the wall. She squinted and tried to focus on it, to read it. Suddenly her vision cleared and the sign was legible. It simply read The Avadora.

She cried out, "Is there no escape?"

***

The proximity alarms on the Matilda

Jon Gray Lang

clangored with warning. Jacquie scrabbled at the controls to find the cause, but only the void of space lay outside the freighter. Breach alarms went off, but the sensors showed that the internal atmosphere was intact.

Barney's voice came over the comm, "What's out there, Jacq? Alarms on all decks going off like mad!"

"There's nothing out there! I'm getting fire alarms going off all over the boat! Do you see anything?" she commed back.

Derain steadily worked through the alarms and shut them off one by one. "The alarms aren't going off for any reason that I can tell."

There was a stillness to every person on board the ship. Their eyes remained glued to the alarm sensors after the last one was shut off. The always present fear of suffocation and being vented out to space rode hard on the crew.

Luli's voice echoed over the ship's comm, "I'm on my way up, Jacq."

***

Galena slowly opened her eyes and stared up at the ceiling of the med lab. Her gaze fell to her body on the operating table and slid over to Anton as he napped in a chair nearby. She pushed herself up until her legs draped over the edge of the table.

The sickbay was dark and silent

except for Doc. The automaton had been brought back online while she had been unconscious. Out past the plas-glass doors, row after row of her sisters flowed through the dance routines she had taught them. Doc bleated forlornly but made no move toward her.

A hand wrapped slowly around her wrist. She spun and yanked her arm outward. The bridge of her hand slammed into a man's jaw. Once her wrist was released, she curled that hand into a fist and swung it into her attacker's cheekbone.

Anton cried out after the second strike, "Stop! No more! No more! Aah!" He backpedaled and flipped over the chair he had slept in.

"Rabbit? Is that you?" Galena murmured in the dark.

Anton felt along his jaw when her fingers enclosed his and pulled him to his feet. "Uh yeah, that would be me, alright." He clicked his jaw left to right. "Damn, you're fast." He could barely make out the ghostly grin that flashed across her face. "By the way, how do you feel? You passed out while you were working on Doc. We thought we might've lost you."

"Did I? Guess that explains why I'm still here." She wandered over and settled next to him. "I had the strangest dream. What did I miss?"

He snorted, "You didn't miss much. What did Luli call it? Oh yeah, just your sisters trying out for a Bugsy Berkeley picture and the

Matilda losing her mind. Seems to be all the rage for our mechanical mates these days." He ignored the whirrs and clicks that emanated from Doc. "Just about every alarm system tripped at the same time. Lu's struggling to figure that out while Barney's been working on that data drive found in Doc."

"Oh." She studied their entwined fingers, "Any clue where we are yet?"

His expression went glum, "Yeah, about that. Looks like a nuke was dropped on the planet below us. There's nothing left down there, just dust and lost memories." A half-hearted smile crossed his face, "We got the probes launched, though. We haven't gotten anything back yet, but it can't be much longer. Right?"

She stared off into the distance. He shrugged and enjoyed this quiet moment with her in the dark sickbay.

Abruptly, she felt along his belt and asked, "Let me see your gun."

"What?"

"Your sidearm. Let me see it. Aah!" she crowed in excitement as she pulled it free of its holster. She quickly got up and hastened over to the empty operating table.

He followed her over and watched as she disassembled his pistol with the skill of a person who had handled it from birth.

"Balance is off. It's definitely going to pull to the right." Her brow quirked as she glanced back at him, "But you're left-handed, so

Jon Gray Lang

you're compensating for that." The outer slide dropped to the table with a thunk. She pulled the barrel and slipped a pinky finger inside it. "Tight coils on the magnetics. This thing'll throw a slug fast and hard."

"I like a sidearm that packs a lot of wallop in a package most won't expect," he grinned.

The pistol housing dropped to the table as the magazine was snatched up. She stripped the first few rounds out and rubbed her fingers against the tips. "You do notch them! But that would cut their effectiveness against armor." Her green eyes glinted as she gazed at him, "Why do you do that?"

He pointed around, "We're on a ship traveling in an airless vacuum. I'd rather not breach the hull by accident."

"Makes sense," she replied matter of factly. She handed his pistol back, completely reassembled, "That's an odd build you've got there, Rabbit."

"It's the closest I've been able to build to what my father trained me with... before he disappeared." He followed her back to the crate and flopped next to her.

"Your father? A familial relationship I can never have." The green of her eyes stared deeply into his, "Would you tell me about him?"

"I guess so." His lids quivered as he wandered back through his memories, "For a long while, it was just me and him. We never really stayed in the same place for very long because we were constantly on the move. I didn't know why when I was little. I just figured everybody did this, that it was normal. But it wasn't. When he thought I was old enough to understand, he told me bad people were after him." His eyes clouded for a moment, "Sometimes the two of us would run off in the middle of the night. We would leave everything behind. But he always kept that gun on him."

A half-smile flickered across his lips, "He would say to me, Henon will protect us. Because thunder is the sound of his voice and those who stand against us will fall to the lightning that Ole Henon here dispenses." Anton held the pistol in his hands as one thumb stroked the slide, "Never forget that, Anton. Never forget."

"And I never did. In fact, I've carried a version of Henon with me ever since." He was reflective for a moment as he slid the pistol back into its holster. "But he was wrong. One day, Henon did fail him and it was just me after that. No one left to give two shits about me." His hands twitched at the memory.

He stared into her face and he could've sworn that her eyes went blacker than ink in the dim light. Her voice rang with a deadness, "All that surrounds us is loss."

***

Barney glanced up from the data

drive in his hands when reports started pouring in from one of the probes. He checked and double-checked the readings before a whoop of excitement burst from him. He bolted over to the comm and keyed it for the entire ship, "The probes have picked up what looks like a jump gate on the outskirts of the system! We can find out where in the nine hells we are and get back home!"

fourteen

Amen

The crew was locked in deep discussion with the genorg leaders when Galena and Anton entered the lounge. Jacquie made quick eye contact with the two of them before she brought the various conversations to a halt. Galena paused in the hatchway a moment before she settled into a seat at the table.

"Barney, bring us up to date."

"Yes ma'am, Captain."

His finger traced over the glowing icon on the table screen. A chart of the local system blossomed across the table, "We were able to assemble this from the probes." He expanded an outer quadrant of the grid and highlighted two points, "Luli has plotted the course to the jump gate and it's loaded up. We've pinged the station beacon and just like everything else in this system, there's no response. But, as we all know, looks can be deceiving. We're going to need to get a team over to the command center on the station and pull the system records. Derain, is the Waratah prepped for launch?"

"She's ready to fly once we're within range," Derain confirmed.

Gamma added, "A squad of my soldiers has volunteered to accompany him."

"More eyes and more guns are never a bad thing," said Anton.

"Remember, we're all in this together. Keep your eyes open for anything that could be used for station or system ident." Jacquie cleared her throat, "Everyone, be careful out there. Don't risk your lives on this. We just need to know where we are."

The genorg commanders left the table with Derain to discuss their roles in the coming operation. Galena got up and walked over to Anton, but he glanced at her apologetically and followed Derain out through the hatch. She turned and found Jacquie talking with Luli. Galena stepped over to her and asked, "What do you need me to do?"

"You? I need you to get better. We've had to replace those stitches a couple of times already. Your wounds aren't completely healed and you're no good to us dead. Now, if you'll excuse me," Jacquie followed Luli and Barney out of the lounge.

Galena looked around at the empty room, "Now what do I do with myself?"

***

Luli grabbed the back of the pilot's chair and plopped down into the hollow while Barney slipped into the seat at the comm station. Jacquie checked down the hall before she swung the hatch closed to the bridge.

She pulled up the chair to the nav station and eyed Barney, "Okay, tell me what you've found."

Barney pulled out his data pad and keyed in a passcode. Once the file he was searching for popped up, he motioned to Luli and Jacquie. They both crouched in.

"I've pulled everything I could off that data drive left in one of Doc's old ports. The protocol was simple but very specific. If Lieutenant Chadov flat lines, inject subject with tube twelve."

"Now Galena opened up that tube and it was loaded with the blue dust we found with Mr. Leon's gear when he was on board," affirmed Luli. "Tests showed that it's designed to interact with the human brain in analytical thought."

Jacquie inquired, "Why would he want to put that crap into her if she was dying?"

"That's the million mazuma question now, isn't it?" muttered Barney.

Jon Gray Lang

Luli followed with, "And we don't have an answer."

Jacquie rubbed her temples in consternation. "I want to keep the Lieutenant out of the loop for now. We don't know what we're dealing with and I don't know if we can fully trust her. Never mind that she scared the hell out of me in the lounge."

"Anton mentioned that she's been acting strangely after she came to from her last collapse," said Luli.

"Keep an eye on her, alright?" Jacquie unknotted her hands, "Next question, where do we stand with Doc?"

"I believe we can reintegrate him with Matilda's systems. I've run multiple tests on his coding and they keep showing clear," Barney stated.

"Good. Hand off that task to the Lieutenant. It'll keep her busy and off the bridge." The Captain tapped the armrest for a moment, "Which means I'm going to need you up here, Barney."

"Got it." He keyed the comm over to the lounge, "Are you still in there, Galena?"

"Yes?"

"I need you to finish up the work on Doc and get him reconnected. Think you can do that?"

"Piece of chicken."

Luli giggled in the background as Barney smiled sardonically, "Barney out."

Jon Gray Lang

fifteen

Ringo Bushi

Galena quickly reassembled Doc's injection arm assembly while she kept an ear open for the comm.

"Cho lo? Cho lo te?" quipped Doc.

Galena thumped his chassis. "Shush you! We'll get you reconnected to Matilda at some point, but not yet."

"Cho lo...?" it chirruped again.

Her eyes rolled as she clipped in the last medical cartridge. She studiously ignored his questioning trills while she reattached the injection assembly to Doc's frame. His chirrups came more frequently and gained in volume.

She whacked him with a wrench, "No, not right now. Shut up!"

In the all too brief silence, Jacquie's

voice came over the comm, "Jump Gate is in range. Permission to launch is granted."

***

Anton kept an eye out through the bow port of the Waratah as it shot free of the Matilda's hangar bay. When the troop carrier spun on its axis and changed direction, he could just barely make out the station lock in the distance. As they floated closer to their objective, he nudged Derain and pointed in its direction.

Derain gave a nod back. He tapped at the attitude jets and the ship's course altered to line up with the airlock. He killed the engines and the ship's momentum carried it the rest of the distance. Anton gave a thumbs up to the six troopers strapped down onto the two benches in the back of the small ship. Once he received six tentative thumbs up in response, his laugh rang out over the open comm.

Derain glared at him before he tripped the ship to ship comm, "Are you getting any readings from the station?"

"Still dead," Barney's voice came back over. "Mmm, poor choice of words. Nothing yet."

Jacquie cut in, "We're keeping all sensors open with weapons hot. Keep in touch."

"Message received, Waratah out," Derain responded.

The Waratah slid toward the station

until Derain hit the attitude control. The ship flipped its trajectory and ran parallel with the large station. She glided along the outer edge while her bow lights played across the pockmarked surface.

Minor surface damage littered the hull that could easily be attributed to such astronomical objects as meteors and dust. There wasn't anything obvious to the eye to explain why the station was quiet until the lights hovered over the airlock.

The outer hatch was simply gone. The entrance shaft had been ripped open. The twisted metal sparkled in the light. Derain angled his vessel until it was perpendicular to the airlock. As the bow lights flickered over the shaft, they could all see that the inner hatch had been bent in half. Flotsam glittered down the hallway and disappeared into darkness.

"Airlock is open to space, both inner and outer," Anton stated into the ship's comm. "We'll have to remain fully suited." There were nods behind him.

"Copy that. Keep an eye open. Matilda will keep you in sight," Jacquie replied.

Derain's grunt came over the ship to ship comm as he pitched the Waratah's trajectory until it faced away from the airlock. The decking reverberated with the launch of the boarding harpoons. Once the solid lock message lit up, he unstrapped himself and declared, "No time like the present."

***

Galena closed her eyes after the latest update. The team had boarded the station. She tried to picture them floating toward the airlock, but the long corridors of the Avadora would spring to mind instead. She convulsed to shake herself free, but there was no escape until her eyes opened.

The vision faded and the sound of her ragged breathing echoed in the empty sickbay. She was glad she wasn't out there with them. It took a moment before she felt calm enough and reattached the outer plate of the assembly. "Check that for me, will you Doc?"

The machine was strangely quiet as it went through a battery of tests. The arm with the injector assembly executed a series of motions before it came to a stop. A chirp of approval resonated from the chassis as the arm tucked itself back into its storage position. A questioning tone came from Doc.

Galena smirked at the automaton, "I'll reconnect you momentarily."

She walked over and clicked the dangling cord into the housing on his chassis. The lights on Doc's board lit up and flickered madly while whirs and pings went off like firecrackers. Abruptly, the lights cut out.

***

Jon Gray Lang

"Whoa!" escaped Luli's lips as her mental connection to the ship died. She pulled the visor away from her face and tried to locate Jacquie in the sudden darkness, "Did you lose connection too?"

Barney stared up at the ceiling and shushed them both. "Life support is off. Bad. This is bad!" He was already in motion as he stood up. He ran out through the hatch only to slam into the far wall and float away. "Damn! Looks like we've lost everything!"

***

"Hello? Matilda, you there? Hello?" Anton thumped his helmet, but the static didn't clear. He switched back to the group comm channel, "I lost communication with the ship. Any of you still have it? No?" His gaze slid along the surrounding walls of the hallway, "Must be something with this station."

He brushed a few empty shell casings out of the way as he followed the last two soldiers down through the empty corridor. Blast marks colored the walls and the few partially intact hatches they passed were either torn open or ripped through. With a short prayer, he checked that Henon was still in his quick-draw holster and the clasp on his knife was still closed.

On their trip down the corridor to the main lift of the station, they found only detritus.

One of the soldiers pushed the floating doors to the lift out of the way. With the lack of gravity, they slowly ricocheted off the walls and tumbled down the corridor in both directions.

Derain clicked the group comm, "We should head straight for the command center. No need to tour the whole place."

"The sooner we get what we came for, the sooner I'm out of here. Lead on, chief," Anton groused.

Derain pointed up the lift shaft. Two of the genorg troops nodded then shut off their magnetic boots. They launched themselves upwards into the darkness. Derain kept an eye on the beams from their flashes as they floated up the shaft.

"All clear," came over the comm.

Derain, followed by two more soldiers, shot up the shaft and caught up with the first two. Only one of the lift doors at this floor had been opened and he helped push the other one back into its slot. By the time they were done, Anton and the rest had joined them.

"This place is spooky, huh?" Anton whispered as he nudged the first body they had come across on the station and pushed it out of the way.

Derain pointedly ignored him as he swung his flash over the station diagram bolted to the wall. He waved to the left and held up three fingers. The forward guard hastened down the hallway and stopped at the third entrance. An "All clear" came over the comm, but Derain hesitated. Anton made a noise and shot down the hall after the two soldiers.

"Duck!" yelled Derain over the comm.

Anton spun around mid-flight at the command. Derain shot a few projectiles past the two genorgs who brought up the rear. The open comm channel filled with screams and shouts when the hallway lit up from the exploding rounds.

Anton flipped head over heels and caught sight of a scuffling, misshapen version of a man reach out for one of the soldiers at the third hatch. Henon flew into his hand and it was back in its holster before the guard even registered the muzzle glow. As he rocketed toward them, he grabbed at her shoulder and shoved her away. She whirled quickly, but the man-like creature had already fallen backward with its neck ruptured.

"I see three more," came over the comm, but Anton couldn't figure out which trooper had said it. He engaged his magnetic boots and clicked onto a wall. His body was yanked sideways when he came to an abrupt halt. Two of the soldiers who had been behind him had already clicked to the decking in kneeling positions and fired a salvo down the hallway. Two more troopers shot past him, followed closely by Derain. Rabbit released his boots from the wall. With a quick spin and push, he helped the last guard to arrive carry her sister in through the third hatch.

Derain manually cycled the hatch closed. A genorg trooper blasted a hole through the faceplate of their wounded member as he turned around.

Anton screamed, "No!"

"She was already contaminated," rang the matter of fact answer through the comm.

Derain floated over to the command station and searched along the edge of the flat surface. "See if you can find a power switch for this thing," he growled.

Two of the women took up guard positions at the hatchway. Another one helped Anton up while the remaining two searched for the junction box. Once it was found, the command station lit up the room with a sickly greenish light. Suddenly, the floor tremored from a heavy impact. Everyone looked toward the hatch.

"They're trying to get in," one of the guards at the hatch stated.

"Derain? This is bad! This is real bad!" Anton shouted.

***

"This is bad, Jacquie! This is really bad!" shouted Barney as he pulled the boots to his spacesuit on. The lights flickered and then came up strong. With one boot on and the other partially hanging off, he hop-struggled back to the bridge. He stopped in his tracks as Anton's voice came over the comm.

"Matilda. Repeat Matilda, are you there? I don't think they can hear us."

Jacquie blew out a pent up breath and clicked the comm switch, "We read you, Rabbit. We lost power for a while..."

"We're under attack!" Anton interrupted. "We made it to the command center, but we're hard-pressed in here. Derain's ransacking the database right now..."

The comm cut off. Jacquie swiped through the comm channels to find a cause. "Barney!"

"On it!" he shouted as he dove under the communication console and ripped the plating out of the way.

***

"Hello? Hello? Damn it! I lost them again," Anton exclaimed as another impact shook the deck.

Derain muttered quietly to himself as he scrolled through the screens of the command station. He spoke over his shoulder, "Try line of sight. You might be able to see them through the port."

"Oh. That's a great idea." Anton stepped gingerly over to the viewport and could just make out the shape of the Matilda against the starry background. "Matilda? Can you hear me? Matilda?

Can any of you hear me?"

***

Galena scurried up to the bridge hatch. What she beheld was a pair of short legs that stuck out from under the comm station. Positioned above them was the Captain as she stabbed her finger repeatedly into the touch screen. Luli was over in the pilot's chair with wires dangling from behind her ear while her hand rested loosely on the visor.

"What's going on?" Galena asked as she stepped in.

Barney's voice reverberated under the station panel, "Not us, Jacq. Must be on their end."

"Matilda? Can any of you hear me? Hello?" Anton's voice shot over the comm.

"They're back!" cried Luli. She looked confused after she pressed the visor hard over her eyes, "What?"

"We can hear you, Anton. You said you're under attack?" Jacquie asked.

"You got it. We've got a hatch between us and them right now, but they want in. And in a bad way." He paused to catch his breath, "The soldiers think that it's contaminated crew members trying to get us. I, I have to agree with them, Jacq. From what I saw, they looked a lot like those things on Ninguiz."

Fear rippled across Jacquie's brow.

Jon Gray Lang

Luli's voice popped up, "You guys aren't going to believe this, but Matilda has a lot of records on the Avadora."

"Not right now, Lu," Jacquie called out.

Barney stood up and wiped his hands on his legs. He looked odd with his spacesuit tied off at his waist and his tools poking out in a ring around his belly.

"I'm trying to get Matilda to stop with the information dump, but she won't leave off," Luli grumbled.

Derain's voice came through the comm, "I finally found it, Jacq. We're in the Lepori..."

"Derain! Please repeat," implored the Captain.

"Leporis system. I repeat; we're in the Leporis system." Derain's voice trailed into static.

Luli glanced up confused, "Leporis? I thought this system was thriving..." Her expression changed from bewildered to frantic as she cried out, "No! No, no, no..."

***

Derain bounded over and joined Anton at the viewport in the control center. Abruptly, a spiraling iris forged of colors ranging between dark purple and blue opened up around the

Matilda. Orange lightning exploded outward to surround the little ship. Anton's gloved hands slapped against the viewport glass as Luli's voice came over the comm, "No, no, no, no..."

His hands fell limply to his sides as the Matilda melted into itself, followed by the iris that had surrounded it dissipating into the night sky.

Derain and Anton turned and gaped at each other. They both felt the eyes of the five troopers on them. Shock and dismay rocked everyone in the command center. They all stared back out the viewport and then at each other.

In disbelief, Anton whispered, "They just left us on an abandoned jump gate in a dead system?"

"Well shit," Derain and Anton said in unison.

sixteen

Undone in Sorrow

The Lieutenant stared out the bow port into the gyrating madness of another uncontrolled jump. The ship had been swallowed whole by the tempestuous storm. While Luli and Barney argued over what to do and Jacquie yelled for a way out, Galena simply stood there and gazed deeply into the waves of shifting colors. The only thought that occupied her mind was that Rabbit had been left behind.

They had left him in a dead system with no escape. He and the others only had a small ship without jump capabilities. She was as still as a statue while the rest of the crew argued around her. There was nothing to do. Nothing to do... but wait.

Jacquie shouted for the fourth time, "Shut up!" After the crew stewed in the silence, she

Jon Gray Lang

reiterated her simple question, "What just happened?"

Luli wiped her sweaty hands on her pant legs before she finally spoke, "The Matilda jumped."

Jacquie rolled her eyes and pointed out the bow port, "I can see that."

"No. I mean the Matilda made the jump. She jumped without receiving any commands from us. She did it on her own." Luli shook her head in confusion, "I don't know how."

Jacquie held off a moment, "So there might be a final destination. Do we know where we're going?"

"She's blocking my access right now. Matilda is, I mean." Luli was quite flustered. "The jump sequence was run once we found out which system we were in. So we've got a destination, I just can't say where," her voice trailed off.

"I'll take any positives I can get right now. Okay, Barney, this one is on you. Should my boat be able to make a jump without our input?"

"No."

She waited for more from him, but he just shrugged his shoulders. Out of the corner of her eye, she spied Galena blankly staring out the bow port, lost in the moment. "Lieutenant? Do you have anything to add?"

Galena slowly turned at the voice that called to her. "Is this real?" she wondered. She focused on where the voice came from until the

Captain's face burst into focus. *'She doesn't trust me, bubbled to the surface of her mind.'* "I brought Doc online, then I came up here."

She watched as the Captain twisted and turned every single phrase she had uttered in search of a separate meaning in them. *'Do I trust myself?'*

***

Derain returned to the command station while Anton checked on the hatch. Unlike most of the hatches they had seen, this one was barely damaged. He placed his gloved hand against its surface and could just make out the small tremors of something or many somethings pounding away at it. His hand dropped to the butt of his gun. His head drooped as he strode past the soldiers on his way back to the bounty hunter. Their faces were lit with a determined yet fatalistic expression he had seen one too many times in the past.

'It's the face you make when you know you're going to die, but you aren't going down without a fight.' And he had to agree. Sure, they had a ship, but it couldn't leave this system.

The only way to get back to the Waratah was past that hatch and those things that wanted in. On top of all that, they had only so much canned air. One of the genorgs must have also figured that part out as she stripped the tank off the dead one. The one they had executed;

maybe the luckiest one in the bunch. Hopelessness began to set in.

"I think I can turn the jump gate on," said Derain.

Anton perked up, "You sure?"

The annoyance from Derain slapped him in the face. "No, I'm not sure. Do you have a better idea or something else to do?"

"Well no..."

"Then come over here and help me out," Derain snarled.

One of the soldiers at the hatch raised her hand, "Excuse me, sirs. Prior to my conscription, I was trained as a jump gate technician."

"See? Why couldn't you be this helpful?" Derain gave Anton the evil eye before he addressed the soldier, "What level? You know what? I can't tell you guys apart. What's your designation?"

"I am Alpha-17."

"The rest of you?" he asked.

Slowly the other four rattled off their designations.

"So, three Alpha models, one Chi and one Delta?" Derain pointed to them individually, "Alright then, you are Alice, you are Anne and you are Agnes. You are Carla and you are Daphne. Anton, write those names on their suits, would you?" He collected his thoughts, "Now which one of you was a gate technician?"

"That would be me."

Jon Gray Lang

Derain just stared at her.

"Uh, I would be Alice?"

"Okay Alice, what level gate technician were you?" he muttered.

"Only entry-level, sir."

Derain turned back to the command station and waved her over. "It's a start."

***

"We're definitely heading somewhere, she just won't let me know where," Luli grumbled as she shoved the visor away from her face.

Barney glumly stated, "I'm not having much luck on my end, either. Looks like I'm going to have to crawl down to her brain and directly connect to her."

"Want me to join you?" Luli asked.

"No, I'll need you up here."

Galena stepped back onto the bridge with lunch and hot drinks on a tray. "I can go with you, Barney."

"Oh, food!" cried Luli as she grabbed a drink and a bowl. She made a kissy face, "Ms. Chadov, I think I love you."

Barney ambled over and grabbed a bowl and cup. "I may take you up on that lass, but I'll have to check with Jacq first. Aah, this smells excellent by the way."

She shrugged as she set the tray down. "I don't have the right skill set for this situation, so I did what I thought would be useful."

"Well, you did right," Luli murmured around a mouthful of wholesome food.

Galena looked around, "Was the Captain with you guys? I didn't see her in the lounge."

"She went down to her cabin. She needed some thinking time away from distractions. Distractions like us," Barney muttered as he took a sip. "She should be awake. I bet you she's hungry, too."

"Okay, thanks." Galena smiled as she picked up the tray and headed out. Once on the lift, she waited until the doors opened on the third deck. She knocked three times on Jacquie's cabin hatch before she announced herself. "Captain? It's me, Galena. I made you some soup."

"Come in."

She swung the hatch open and found Jacquie hunched up on her bunk with her data pad in hand. Galena set the tray down, closed the hatch and handed her the cup.

Jacquie mumbled, "Thanks."

She flopped next to the Captain on the bed and poked her with a forefinger. Jacquie started in surprise. She looked back down at her data pad and then set it aside. A playful pout crossed her face, "And what can I do for you, Lieutenant?"

Galena handed her the bowl, "Eat this before it gets cold." She nestled her hands in her lap, "Anton says that this soup is terrible when cold."

"He would," she said after a spoonful. "Of course, he'd be right. Mmm. This is really good!"

Galena watched as Jacquie wolfed down the bowl. "Captain? You've been avoiding me."

"No I haven't," Jacquie mumbled defensively around a mouthful of liquid comfort.

But Galena continued, "And you've cut me from being any use on your ship."

"Well, you've been hurt and I want you to get..."

Galena placed her finger over Jacquie's lips. She waited until Jacquie took the hint. "I am not a weak thing, Jacq. I was designed for labor. I was built to work every day until I could work no more. Until I simply stop functioning." Her arms spread outward, "I am not built for this. This doing nothing." She dropped her hands in her lap, "You won't involve me in what's going on. The others won't give me anything to do without your say so. Let me help. Give me something to do."

Jacquie stared into those green eyes that held her gaze. She looked away and preoccupied herself with finishing the soup. She placed the bowl back onto the tray and turned back to the Lieutenant. "You are correct. I have been purposely cutting you out of the loop. And it's not that I think you're weak. It's that I have too many questions involving you."

"Questions? What questions?"

Concern lit Jacquie's eyes as she stared at her. "You were infected on board that ship by Tom-knows-what. Which should have changed you. And yet, you're still you, most of the time. Furthermore, you have a piece of illegal tech embedded in your brain. Somehow that chip-set is preventing the affliction from spreading. And last but not least, our friend Mr. Leon hijacked my med bot into injecting you with some drug that was primed for the moment that you would die."

Galena's eyes widened and she fell back in shock.

"And back to the major complication; you aren't you all of the time." Jacquie stabbed her in the chest with her finger, "Sometimes when you talk to us, you're not there. It's as if something else inhabits your body, staring back at us through your eyes." She glared at Galena, "And that something scares me."

"I was contaminated?" Galena's memories of the genorg troops on the ship sprang to mind. "But how can that be?"

"Ever since Luli dragged your carcass back on board the Matilda, you've been nothing but a series of question marks." Jacquie rubbed her temples, "I only wish I had prevented you from entering that cursed ship."

Galena sat back on the bed and her brow wrinkled, "Knowing that helps. It's strange. I still have dreams that I'm trapped on board the Avadora." She whispered, "I struggle with the thought that all of this is the dream and I never really left that ship. That I never escaped it." She swung back around to Jacquie. "And that's why I need something to do! To help me get away from there."

Jacquie tried to ignore the pleading expression on Galena's face, but she understood. Dark memories are like traps. They are hard to escape and they leave you in the worst places you can imagine.

Her shoulders bowed under the weight of her own memories, "We'll figure something out." But she wondered how she would keep this promise.

seventeen

Old Ship of Mine

"There's got be a way to get out of here." Anton slapped at the command console.

Alice scrolled through the jump gate command screens, "We could always complete the evacuation protocol."

"What do you mean evacuation protocol?" asked Anton.

"What do you mean complete?" Derain queried.

Alice looked at both men before she settled on Derain. Anton threw his hands up in frustration and leaned against the bulkhead.

"The evacuation protocol gets activated when a system is listed as a danger to the whole of the Consortium. To block access to and from that system, the gate station would be destroyed." She pointed to the screen, "See here? It was activated, but then the process was interrupted."

Derain glanced at the blinking warning light she pointed to, "And how does destroying the station help us?"

Anne's voice came over the comm, "The hatch isn't going to hold out for much longer."

"Thank you for the update," Derain replied. He stared at Alice and waited for an answer.

Alice looked confused. "The protocol includes an emergency jump for gate personnel prior to its detonation?"

"Now see? That's a good answer. I like an actual answer to a problem," Anton rambled.

Derain glared at Rabbit until he quieted. "We were not aware of that, Alice. Please continue."

Alice cleared the warning and keyed through the menu. She pulled up the destination request screen, "Where would we want to go?"

"Farla's only a gate away," Anton offered. "Let's go there."

"Ignore him. Set it for Erebus," Derain commanded.

Anton's bafflement was legible through his faceplate, "Why there? That's a backwater system."

"Jacquie and I chose Erebus for a rendezvous in case we ever got separated," Derain replied. "The problem, in this case, is going to be the when of it."

"The when of it?" Anton muttered.

Alice finished entering the port of call and completed the remaining steps of the protocol. A claxon rang through all the open communication channels.

Anton jerked at the sound. "The alarms are going off. Why are the alarms going off?"

"I set the destination and ran the evacuation protocol as you requested," Alice responded.

"Warning! Warning! All personnel have twenty minutes to evacuate the station!" broadcast on all the comm channels.

"No time like the present then," Anton muttered as he slipped his knife free and unholstered Henon.

Derain wanted to rub his temples. Even knowing he would die if he removed his helmet didn't stop the desire. "I'm probably going to die anyway at this rate. Surrounded by idiots and monsters. And I don't know which is worse." He faced the only exit, "Okay. You four, cover that hatch. Alice? To me. Rabbit, you're on door duty."

The genorg soldiers formed up a firing line on the right while Derain and Alice took the left flank. Anton hopped over to the latch and waited for the nod from Derain. With a practiced motion, he dropped the lever and yanked the hatch open. He fell back as what had once been the crew of this station stumbled their way in.

The first few were decimated by the withering fire from the troopers. But as more of them poured in, their numbers simply overwhelmed the entrance and spilled over to the sides.

"Warning! Warning! All personnel have fifteen minutes to evacuate the station!"

Anton plunged his knife into the skull of a being that was more ghoul than man and it collapsed under the force of the impact. "We're running out of time, folks! We need to make a break for it!" He wrenched his knife free and Henon clicked on an empty chamber. "How the hell are these things alive in a vacuum?"

Derain knew he was right. They had to get out of here soon or they'd go up with the station. He kicked one of the attackers away and brought his pistol up, but it also cycled to an open chamber. He stomped on the head of what had once been an attractive woman when a lull appeared in the hatchway. The time to get a move on was now.

"Everybody! Move! Move! Move!" Alice's rifle butt flashed past Derain's helmet and struck an attacker he had missed. "Go for broke! Run to the airlock! Agnes, Daphne, grenades!"

They bunched up at the hatch and launched themselves down the hallway. Two grenades were tossed back on their way out and went off in brief, but bright flashes. Anton howled when he crashed body first into some debris. Carla,

Anne, and Alice shot past him, followed closely by Derain. He untangled himself in time as Agnes and Daphne shot by. They rolled through the lift opening and disappeared from his sight. With a quick glance over his shoulder, he spied some movement, quite a lot of movement headed his way.

"Get a move on, Rabbit! What are you waiting for?" he cursed as he launched himself down the lift shaft. The flash beams of the team were swallowed up as they exited the lift. Suddenly, a hand grabbed his leg. He twisted around as he was dragged to a standstill. His knife bit into the fingers but the creature refused to release him. His flash illuminated the eyes, black as pitch, dark as night, and eternal as time while they stared emptily back at him.

"Warning! Warning! All personnel have ten minutes to evacuate the station!"

"I don't have time for this!" Anton sawed the fingers off and kicked himself loose. With a quick push off the wall, he accelerated down the shaft. His body shot through the lift entrance, where he caught himself on his hands and shoved off. His magnetic boots engaged and clicked to the ceiling. A quick search showed Derain waving them on from far down the hallway. A sudden bright flash from behind startled him. Carla flew past and debris rained against his back. Deep vibrations rattled the ceiling plates, so he launched himself after her. "We're running out of time! The jump gate generators just kicked on!"

Jon Gray Lang

"Then move faster!" shouted Derain as he came to the blasted airlock. His heart lifted when he could make out the Waratah floating out there, still tethered to the station. A shudder passed through him when he spied a man-shaped thing crawling on the hull.

A trooper landed next to him and looked over her shoulder, "Shouldn't be much longer, sir."

He glanced down at her and the name Anne was scrawled in greasepaint across her chest plate, "Thank you, Anne. Would you be so kind as to get that thing off my ship?"

He kept one eye on it as she brought up her rifle, fired and re-slung it to her back. The target stiffened before it let go of the troop carrier and floated off into space. "Let's get out of here."

The two of them launched themselves toward the Waratah. Daphne and Agnes landed at the edge of the torn metal of the airlock, followed shortly by Alice. They linked up and propelled themselves toward the ship.

"Warning! Warning! All personnel have five minutes to evacuate the..."

Anton caught most of the message as he flew out toward Derain's ship and out of broadcast range. Carla barreled past him, grabbed his suit and yanked him into the vessel. Derain released the harpoons and the troop transport began to float away from the doomed station. With a hit to the attitude jets, the Waratah maneuvered its way toward the scaffold ring of the jump gate. The spinning vortex tugged at the little ship.

Derain shouted over the comm, "Everyone! Strap down!"

Carla strapped herself in as Anton pulled himself over the copilot's chair and plunked down in it. He jerked back in surprise as a grotesquerie of a man slammed into the bow port and scrabbled for a handhold. It was quickly followed by another and then another of the deformed beings.

The bent and twisted man-things leapt out of the station airlock and smacked against the troop transport. Derain ignored them and lined up the Waratah with the center of the whirlpool.

The gravitational force hurled the ship into the eye of the storm and a wave of disorientation struck the vessel. The creatures still attached to the hull immediately pulped, then disintegrated into motes of crystalline dust. When the wormhole finally stretched out all around them, Derain relaxed visibly.

After the ship exited the wormhole and passed through the gate of the Erebus system, Anton muttered, "Huh. I always wondered what that would do to a person."

***

Galena studied a three-dimensional image that hovered in front of her of the implanted chip-set inside her skull. She compared the medical scan from her first time on the Matilda to the scan run right after Luli had brought her back. She pulled another digital image and her finger tapped against her temple.

Barney came up beside her and peered at the image, "I haven't seen this one."

"I just ran it an hour ago." She pointed at a discolored blotch on the image, "Do you see that? The implant is spreading. It's following the brain stem down through the spinal cord." A frustrated sigh escaped her, "But what is it? Where did it come from? And what's it doing inside of me?"

She grabbed the toxicology report and pointed to an entry marked by a blinking 'NOT FOUND' icon, "And this stuff? At least I know it must have come from that damn ship. But why is the tech in my brain interacting with it?" She wondered out loud, "Was all this planned in some way? Am I some kind of experiment?"

Barney took the data pad from her hand and set it down. "I don't know, but we'll figure it out." He patted her hand lightly, "But right now I need the help you offered. Are you up for it?"

"Yes," she replied instantly. "I am up for anything other than this. What are we going to do?"

"Why we're going to visit the mind of Matilda. You, uh, might need a helmet."

***

Luli pulled back from the visor and grabbed a drink from the small cold box. Her head settled in the cradle of the chair and she closed her eyes. "Matilda is obsessed with trying to remember that cursed ship, the Avadora. I've gone in there and argued with her about it, but she just keeps rifling through her ghost records looking for any mention of that name. I find the fact that she thinks she remembers the name disconcerting enough, to say the least." Her eyes slit open and a frown graced her lips, "I wish I had never touched those blasted records."

"You and Barney both," Jacquie smirked.

Luli snorted into the quiet and the pressure on the bridge released like an opened valve.

"It's weird, you know? I was excited that she had found something, maybe an answer. But the more we learn, the stranger it gets and the less I want anything to do with it." Luli tossed her data pad into Jacquie's lap, "Take that one, for instance. She finally answered where we're going. Of course, the answer doesn't mean a damn thing. To us, anyway."

"Wait," Jacquie said as she fumbled with the pad, "You got an answer? What was it?"

Luli looked up, "Huh? Oh, she says we're going to the terminal advent. Who knows what the hell that means."

Jon Gray Lang

Jacquie grimaced, "I guess we'll find out soon enough."

"I guess," Luli responded.

The two of them lapsed into their own thoughts. Beyond the Matilda churned an unsettling panorama. Jacquie kept an eye on it while she tapped a fist against her knee.

Somehow the Matilda had forced a jump, which she shouldn't be capable of. Now, the ship's computer was locked deep into its memory banks and bits of information were tossed out piecemeal. Barney and Lu were dealing with the same problem from different angles, but the solution hadn't been forthcoming.

"At this point, we can only hope," Jacquie proclaimed wistfully. Outside the ship, the only movement was the sky itself. Her voice took on a quizzical tone, "Have you noticed how quiet it's been? We haven't been harassed since we jumped."

"That's a good thing, right?"

***

As Galena followed Barney deep into the bowels of the ship, her head slammed into a large crossbeam for what must have been the fifth time. She caught Barney's chuckle and wished for the fourth time that she had taken his advice about a helmet. The access tunnels they traveled through were cramped and the ceilings were low.

"Low for anyone taller than a Titan

that is" she amended.

Galena tried to rub the bruise forming on her forehead away. At this rate, the electronic chip in her skull would be nothing but shards of plastic and metal. She cursed again as the side of her head smacked against a pipe, "Damn the Major! I swear you're trying to kill me!"

Barney kept on chuckling as he stepped over a ventilation shaft. He disappeared around a bend and bellowed, "Well, you can stop grumbling because we're here!"

She sidled up next to him as he removed an outer plate and set it to the side. A heat shield and then an inner plate followed it shortly thereafter. Galena peeked over his shoulder and a confusion of wires, lights and open ports glimmered back at her. "So that is what we're looking for?"

Barney replied, "You've seen the heart of her in the engine room. Now, come gaze upon the brain of this old boat."

His hand reached out and touched it with a grace Galena had not seen from him before, "Oh Matilda, we've been through a lot together, haven't we?" A reckless grin split his face as he motioned toward the Lieutenant, "Now let's crack her open."

Galena found a spot nearby that didn't leave her neck cricked and keyed the portable comm to the bridge, "We made it to the processor casing. We're pulling the plates off right now."

"We're going to interrupt your

scheduled programming!" Barney cried with relish. "I've always wanted to do this." He rubbed his hands vigorously together, "I've finally got the chance to open her up and take a poke around."

Galena shut off the comm and watched him work, "How long do you think this'll take?"

"You in a hurry or something?" He waited for a reply, but the Lieutenant remained silent. "I don't really know since I don't know what I'm looking for." He shimmied to the left and slid an arm further into a dark opening, "Here, hold that in place would you?"

She reached over and pushed against a small sliver of plasteel. He grunted and she heard an audible click. She pulled the sliver out while he freed his arm.

"Barney?"

"Hmm?" he replied.

She asked hesitantly, "The time has never been right or we've been too busy, but..."

He interrupted her, "Go ahead and spit it out, missy."

"Why were your people going to sell you into the sex trade? I don't understand."

To her surprise, he suddenly beamed at her, "Aha! No one can resist that bit of verbal bait." He threw a coquettish pout her way, "Am I not inviting enough to your eyes?" The flustered look she gave him made him burst out in laughter. He wiped a tear from his cheek before his manner sobered, "I am special amongst my people, just as my people are special compared to the other human colonies."

"Special? In what way?"

He rambled over her, "Well, different might be a better way to put it." He fished a cord out of a pocket and plugged it into his data pad, "I guess I should start from the beginning. You see, Titan was an anomaly for colonization. Sure it could grow things and had animal life, but the gravity was too high for humans as they were."

He reached deep into the cavity and popped in the other end of the cord, "Long ago, if the histories are right, a sleeper ship had been directed to the system. Once it arrived, it didn't have enough fuel to go anywhere else. The first generation of my ancestors lived out their lives on the ship and few, if any, ever set foot on the planet. But pragmatism breeds solutions and a solution was found. Here, hold this, will you?"

She took the data pad from his hand as he pulled a set of cords out of his belt pouch. Each one was plugged into a series of open ports. He took the data pad back and scrolled through a sequence of command screens.

"And?" she asked.

He blinked at her for a moment before he continued, "The original colonists decided that their children had to be altered at the genetic level if they were to survive on the high gravity world. Once they reached an adult age, many of them were sent down to the surface. The first generation eventually died out and the second generation bred. Experimentation continued as well. The third and fourth generations were more suited to the environment. Over time, the planet had an impact on my people," he grinned at her, "and my people on it."

An error popped up on the screen, "Hmm, that's weird. Look at this." He held the data pad up to her.

"Matilda is running a new subroutine?" she muttered out loud. She took the device from him, clicked back a few screens and chose a different direction. "No. Not new. Pretty old in fact."

He beamed at her, "Good eye. You've come a long way in such a short time. You'll have this stuff down pat in no time!" He pointed to the screen, "Keep an eye on that."

"What should I look for?"

"A response. Anything odd." He winked at her, "You'll know it when you see it." He rearranged some of the cords and placed them into different ports. "Now where was I? Oh yes. An anomaly, like me, cropped up in the third generation and increased in the fourth generation. By the sixth generation, the aberration, as it was called, leveled out."

Anger colored his tone, "So what did the religion of my people, the only belief structure allowed on the planet mind you, choose to do with those that were affected by the deviance? Why, we must perform our Gods given role to soothe the desires of those in power, be they political, religious or economic." He gave her a grimace, "It wasn't until I escaped that I could even grasp that it was just sanctioned sexual slavery."

"How can natural-borns justify treating one of their own as less than themselves?" She pondered this as she watched the data pad. Suddenly, a line blinked through on the screen and a system schematic appeared, "I just got a response."

"Let me see."

She flipped the data pad toward him and he tracked the line. He reached behind him, switched out some of the cords, but the schematic remained unchanged.

"Here." He spun the screen back and crammed as much of his body under the casing unit as he was able. His fingers reached toward an empty slot and poked around.

Galena stared at the screen and then watched Barney as he changed the ports for some of the cables. Her brow wrinkled, "Barney? I do not understand. What makes you different from the rest of your people?" The line on the schematic blinked out and came back up. "It went dark for a moment."

The Titan backed himself out and grabbed the data pad out of her hands. He considered her for a moment, "I'm a hermaphrodite, Galena. Born that way and reviled for it."

His shoulders shook and his voice grew dusky. An old resentment painted the words as he recited what sounded like a mantra,

"The ancestors who brought us home
made of us what was needed.
Blessed be they who came before us.

They made of us the genders three,
each with its purpose designed.
Blessed be their foresight.

The male and female shall be
the bearers of our future.
Blessed be they who come after us.

The androgyne shall be held
close to the designer's bosom.
Blessed be those who bear the
burden of us."

He poked disconsolately at the data pad in the ensuing silence, "It didn't make much sense to me, but then my family raised me as a single gender." He looked up at her, "Normally, I would've been taken when I was young. They would've kept me illiterate and had me serve God's given purpose until it broke me or killed me. Generally at the hands of those who laid the groundwork for future generations."

"But why would they do that to you?

It doesn't make sense," Galena said quietly.

"I never understood it and neither did my family. I was lucky in that regard. Someone eventually figured out what I was even before I did and my family had me smuggled away for my own safety."

Abruptly, the schematic on the screen lit up. A sickening sense of being pulled apart and put back together again ripped through the pair of them.

Galena could have sworn that she saw a spectral tendril slip along the cabling into Matilda's brain, but then the ship bucked and she lost sight of it. Her shoulder banged against the wall of the service shaft and when she looked again, it was gone.

She cried out, "Did we just jump?"

He started snorting, "Oh, you sneaky old bird. That's how you did it!"

The Lieutenant looked on in confusion as Barney heaved himself to his feet and did a little dance.

"Come on!" he shouted. "We have to get back to the engine room."

"Shouldn't we put this back together?" she asked.

His apparent enthusiasm slipped, "Oh, yes. That would be the proper thing to do."

***

Luli's head smacked into the pilot's visor as the ship shuddered violently. Jacquie spilled out of her chair and tumbled to the bridge decking.

"Did we just jump?" Jacquie asked as she pushed herself up to her feet.

Luli rubbed at the new scrape above her eye. She squinted through the other eye and stars, real stars, filled the window. "Sure looks like it. Now where, in all of space, are we?"

Jacquie ambled over to the nav console while Luli jammed the visor back over her eyes. The pilot's hands played rapidly over the touch screen below. Luli muttered, "Color me surprised, but I got a match."

"Where are we then?" Jacquie asked.

Luli pushed the visor away, "The Tiburon system?"

"Terminal Advent reached," an oddly accented and unknown voice echoed from the nav station. The Tiburon star map flashed across its screen.

Luli and Jacquie stared at the console in surprise. In unison, they said, "Who was that?"

Jon Gray Lang

eighteen

Bold Fisherman

"Mr. Tiwi, there is absolutely no reason to raise your voice to me. I am simply following procedure," replied the desk clerk.

This was the third employee of Transport Customs Bureau the bounty hunter had been forced to deal with. Annoyingly, he wasn't getting very far with anyone on the backwater planet Mithuna of the Erebus system.

Derain tweaked the bridge of his nose. He glanced over to Anton and the five heavily armed genorg troops slouched in a corner, "Should I have them clear the room?"

He shook his head in frustration as he dealt with the brick wall that existed on every planet. The wall, known as bureaucracy. "I don't think you understand, Mr. uh..."

Jon Gray Lang

"For the fifth time, you may refer to me as Mr. Poulos."

"Well, Mr. Poulos, I don't think you understand that I need my ship. It is not my fault that your gate system thinks I came from a quarantined system," Derain harangued.

"I am very sorry, Mr. Tiwi, but your vessel must remain in quarantine for seven solar days. Then, and only then, will you be able to retrieve it," sniffed Mr. Poulos.

"What am I supposed to do in the meantime?"

"I suppose you could do whatever it is your ilk do. Good day, Mr. Tiwi." The man slammed his window shut and left Derain fuming.

He trod past Anton and company with a "Come on" before he disappeared past the door.

Anton shrugged and stood up, "Ladies? If you'll follow me?"

They caught up with the bounty hunter halfway down the street. Anton grabbed him by the shoulder, "Hey. Stop." As he slowed down, Anton simply asked, "What do we do to find Jacq? What's the next step?"

"We wait. Until then, we find a place to stay." Derain went through his wallet, "I'm a little strapped for traveling currency, so maybe find some work, too."

***

With his fingers steepled, Mr. Leon ruminated at the desk of his new office. He had recently arrived on Mithuna and still hadn't gotten used to the higher gravity. His eyes tracked the two suns of this hot planet as they set over the stumpy mountain range. There was a light knock at the door, but he waited until the second sun was swallowed whole by the mountains. "You may enter."

One of his people, a Ms. Kwan, stepped through the door and stood patiently by the corner of his desk. He waved her to a seat and regarded her until she brought forth her data pad.

At his nod, she began, "Sir. As you can see here, one of the ships you requested a monitor on has arrived at the spaceport. The Waratah."

He perked up at the name. It was one of the vessels his brother-selves had requested an eye be kept out for. "Oh? Where is the ship now and where is the crew?"

"The ship was impounded under a quarantine ruling." She scrolled through the file, "The seven members are staying at a dive motel in the Ekaju corridor."

"Seven? Well now, that's interesting." He mulled this over, "Do we have a physical description of the seven?"

Ms. Kwan leaned back a moment with her brow furrowed. She thumbed through the

Jon Gray Lang

screens until a pleased expression lit up her eyes, "I have a series of holo copies of them here, sir." She handed the device to him and relaxed into the leather chair that was easily double her yearly salary.

He perused the holos, one after the other. The bounty hunter he recognized. He also recognized the one time terrorist or revolutionary, depending on which side you had rooted for. But why would they be traveling with what looked like five fifth-generation genorgs outfitted as Consortium troops? In point of fact, why weren't they with the Matilda? He handed the data pad back, "Which ruling was their ship impounded under?"

"Arrival from a quarantined system, sir."

He kept his eyes locked on her until she stuttered, "The Leporis system."

His left eyebrow quirked in surprise, "Leporis? Now, that is quite unexpected." He opened a drawer in his desk, "Thank you, Ms. Kwan. You may go."

As she crested the door, her name was called out. She stopped and turned to her employer.

"Would you be so kind as to leak this information through some of the more nefarious channels of this planet? Let it be known that a certain agitator known as Anton Roane is here on Mithuna. Thank you."

"Of course, sir."

Jon Gray Lang

As she left his office, he turned to look out upon the stars that were just beginning to dust above the mountain tops. "I wonder what sort of fish we'll catch in our net."

In a pique of humor, he sang softly to himself, "There was a bold fisherman who sailed out from Pimlico, to slew the wild codfish and the bold mackerel..."

***

"Hey Captain, we're in line for the gate jump to Erebus. Current estimate is one hour." Luli rolled her eyes, "Who knew today was the main transport shipment date for that crappy little mining colony."

"I sure didn't," quipped Jacquie. "You would think Delta's folks would be antsy by now, but apparently they're used to these long periods of doing nothing." She glanced out the bow port. The jump gate's iris swirled tightly and pulled another ship through before it quieted down. "I am looking forward to some honest to goodness wormhole travel. I don't want to use that contraption down there for a long time. You got that Barney?"

Barney's muffled voice floated up from underneath the pilot console, "I couldn't agree more."

His torso shimmied out into the open and his hands slapped together, "All done. Okay, Lu, any time we want to make a jump, you'll need to flip that toggle switch over there. This goes for any and all jumps."

He grabbed the console and hauled himself up, "You hear me, you tumbling block of a trawler? You can't go gallivanting about without letting us know what the hell is going on or where you're taking us!"

The ship tilted to the aft for a moment before leveling out. "I'm still working on that one," muttered Barney.

"Me too," Luli grimaced as she laid her hand against the starboard bulkhead.

Barney continued muttering out loud, "Repurposing the electrical wiring for your own use. Trying to make a mess of things, you crazy boat..." He looked up at the smirk on Jacquie's face, the quizzical expression on Galena's and Luli giggling behind her hand, "No respect sometimes..."

Jacquie pointedly looked away. "We've got a couple hours to kill, Ms. Qing. What have you been wanting to tell me?"

Luli's face took on a conspiratorial look, "It's about the Matilda and that enigma of a ship. Dun, dun dun! The Avadora."

"You found something useful in those ghost records?" asked Barney.

"More like the Matilda found them for me. They're a little spotty, but it's a bit of a strange tale."

"Oh she's getting all mysterious now," Jacquie quipped with a wink.

Jon Gray Lang

Luli responded in mock surprise, "Why I would never..."

"Wouldn't you?" asked Galena.

Barney laughed, "Yes, you would. Even the Lieutenant gets it, Lu."

Luli acted hurt, "Well, now I don't know if I should."

"But you will," laughed Jacquie.

Luli stuck out her tongue. "Fine. From what I was able to glean, the jump engine was installed some time after the Matilda was retired from active service. She was used as a testbed for short distance experimental jumps. Now, I'm not entirely sure, but the Avadora may have been the testbed for jumps on the bigger engine as well. I can't rightly say because that name is all tangled up in her logs during that period in time. Unfortunately, those records were all wiped from her core." She threw her hands up in frustration, "Which is why we're just left with these fragments."

Barney piped up, "Did you find out where the engines came from or who built them?"

"The only record I came across was that the engines had been listed as recovered from a shipwreck. But there's no information on the wreck. To be honest, I get the feeling that those files originated somewhere outside of Consortium space. I think they might be far older than expected, maybe pre-Consortium entirely."

Luli continued, "Funnily enough, I hadn't really gotten anywhere with those ghost files

Jon Gray Lang

until someone ran that search for the Avadora. Well, Matilda recognized the name and she worked hard on that search. I think this is what may have caused her to make that jump. It's like she panicked."

"Panicked? But she's a ship. Ships don't panic. Right?" asked Galena.

"But if these experimental jumps are from before her arrival in Consortium space, why is Tiburon the Terminal Advent?" wondered Jacquie.

"Isn't that the system she was salvaged from, initially? Maybe it was after a very long jump," Barney pondered. "Were you able to retrieve anything else?"

"Once we came through the jump, I was able to dig up some information on the Terminal Advent." Luli pulled the coordinates of their arrival point and then pulled the records for the Terminal Advent point. "As you can see here, they match. But if you look closer, the Terminal Advent coordinates were partially lost, so she assembled coordinates from what was available."

"So this system is not the Terminal Advent?" asked Galena.

"It sure isn't. At the same time, I don't know what is. Could be a million different combinations..." Luli placed a hand over her ear, "Hold on a moment. Looks like we'll be processed through next."

"Good news," Jacquie stated as she ran her hand through her hair. "I have to give it to Mr. Leon. We wouldn't get through this gate so easily without that mirrored transponder code he gave us." She smiled, "Not that I don't have a few other tricks up my sleeve, but my hand is getting a bit thin."

The crew sat in silence as the ore transporter in front of them shot through the generated wormhole. Once Luli received the go-ahead, she lined up the Matilda as a vortex formed within the confines of the ring. The ship shuddered from the gravitational pull before it yanked them through.

"Erebus, here we come," announced Luli.

"I hope you're there, Derain," prayed Jacquie.

Another Saturday Night

A filthy rivulet of debris-filled water ran along the length of the dank alleyway. Tall buildings blocked out most of the light from the dual suns which left a double layer of shadows. The gang markings that were sprayed randomly on the walls were difficult to see in the middle of the day. It stank of rotting vegetation and human waste. Rabbit did not want to know what he was standing in. He spotted the door they were searching for and headed off in that direction.

"I'm at the rear exit with Agnes. On your call, Derain," Anton whispered into the short-range comm. He threw a quick nod to Agnes as he slid to one side of the door and her to the other. Together, they both drew their weapons and waited. Derain's voice could barely be made out as it echoed down the alley. But the rhythmic pounding of a person running full tilt into the back door was quite audible.

The door slammed open and ricocheted off the wall. The man who bolted through went flying as he tripped over Agnes' foot that she had shoved in the way. Anton leapt on top of the runner as he struggled to get up. He trapped both wrists and locked the restraining bracelets in place. A woman flew out through the open door and bounced off him as she darted off to the left. The low thunk from the genorg's rifle melted into the sudden scream of the woman as she fell to the street in a tangle of legs and trash.

"You got her, Agnes?"

She nodded as he brought the skip up to his knees, "You shouldn't run, my friend."

"You've got the wrong guy! I didn't do nothing!"

"Yeah, you and your crew haven't robbed any local businesses in the past month and a half," Derain wisecracked as he sauntered through the back door. He was quickly followed by the other genorgs with the other culprits in tow.

Anton piped in, "I bet he's never met any of these people. Isn't that right?"

"Yeah, that's it! I don't know any of them."

Carla replied in a deadpan voice, "We are not judges. We only capture those who have a warrant."

Jon Gray Lang

Anton smirked, "Are you developing a sense of humor, Carla?"

Derain chuckled under his breath, "I think she just might be. Let's get these people to the station. No need to keep mazuma wasting in the street."

They walked out of the alleyway and headed off down to the station. Strangely enough, it was less than a couple of blocks away. Rabbit hung back and kept an eye out as the team moved past him.

A smile ghosted on his face. They worked pretty well together. It didn't hurt that they looked like a force to be reckoned with. This was their third tag-n-bag and it had gone off like clockwork. Anton was a little surprised by this, but he had to agree with Derain. This bounty hunting stuff was a decent fit for someone with his skill set.

Their time on Mithuna had been eventful yet smooth; one could say almost fun. The latest update was that the Waratah should be released from quarantine by tomorrow. Even with the ship storage fees, they should have enough mazuma left over to split it out amongst them all. Truth be told, it had been quite a pleasant week.

***

The latest report on the team of bounty hunters arrived on Kwan Sang's data pad. She compiled the information with the previous dailies and tried to find a deeper meaning in it. Mr. Leon had requested a daily update on their actions, but she couldn't understand what it was about them that kept his interest.

As was custom, she waited at the rather ornate door until he invited her in. She took one of the empty seats and he offered her a cup of what could only be coffee. The cost alone in the tiny demitasse was more than her monthly rent. As always, his demeanor and mannerisms seemed slightly contradictory. Her employer was very polite and generally well dressed, but she was unnerved by his gaze. Sometimes it felt as if thousands of eyes were upon her, other times only two. Today it felt like many.

Mr. Leon's head inclined, "Good morning, Ms. Kwan. Any relevant news about our quarry and his merry little band?" He took a dainty sip of his espresso.

She glanced down at her data pad, "There isn't very much, I'm afraid. Their ship is set to be released from quarantine today, as you ordered." She scrolled down, "They've completed their third contract for the local constabulary and are still at the Spring Mountain Motel. That may change once their ship is returned."

"Maybe, maybe not." He steepled his fingers, "Still no bites on our leak? Our trackers haven't spotted anyone following them?"

"They've seen no movement, sir."

The desk comm blinked and Mr.

Leon held up a finger as he answered it. Ms. Kwan gazed placidly out the window until his conversation finished. When she turned back to him, she was a bit surprised to see him beaming with excitement. The caller must have relayed some welcome news.

"I think that may change within the next day or so, Ms. Kwan. You may go now." He waved her toward the door.

Just as she reached it, he called out, "Ms. Kwan, would you send out a squad to watch for an incoming ship?"

She let the door close under its own weight and turned around, "Of course, sir. Which ship?"

"That would be the Matilda."

twenty

In the Aeroplane Over the Sea

"Well, I'm out," Anton grunted as he stood up from the poker game. "You want in, Derain?"

"Oh no," Derain laughed as he looked over the soldiers at the rickety table. "Those ladies are much too sharp for me."

"Ha!" barked Anton. He glanced back and remarked, "Alice, it looks like we'll need to give you a trim when you're done."

She grimaced as she dealt out the next hand, "Understood, sir... I mean, Anton."

It had taken some effort, but Rabbit had convinced the ladies to let him style their hair. He had pushed the idea that with a name came the need for a more individual look. Once the troopers had relented, he had gone into it with gusto. Agnes now sported a short bob, Daphne a Mohawk while Anne's hair had been given a double toned look. The right side of Alice's head was shaved down to the skin and Carla's entire scalp was stubble with geometric patterns cut into it.

When the genorgs had pressed about where he had learned the craft, Rabbit had hemmed and hawed about a previous job and left it at that. But after he surveyed his handiwork, he said it felt good to use some of his old skills. Derain figured it was all to keep busy while they waited on the Matilda's arrival.

The man had also gone out of his way to teach the ladies how to gamble. Derain, on the other hand, had kept to reading an old paper book when he wasn't searching for their next gig.

Daphne took the vacant seat at the table while Anton wandered over and joined Derain in the small kitchenette. "I'm probably going to regret teaching them."

"Probably? You mean you don't yet?"

Rabbit hedged a little before he nodded, "Empty pockets, nothing to lose. That's me." He walked over to the cold box, "Something that will never change apparently. You want a drink? Any of you ladies want something?" He opened the box and pulled out a bottle. "Just me, huh? Must be time to drown my poor man sorrows."

Derain scrolled through the available warrants in the city. "Must be." He glared at the screen and forced himself to relax, "Feels good to have my ship back, though. Now I can do a full planet search for these losers."

"Hey, I used to be one of those losers," Anton muttered.

"What do you mean, used to be?" Derain laughed.

Anton watched the bounty hunter scroll through the warrant list while the cheers and laughter of the game he had recently vacated played out behind them. "Hey, Derain, how long do you think we'll be stuck here?"

"Could be a week; could be a month. Depends on where they ended up." He cleared his throat, "Which we won't know until we see them."

Anton folded his arms, laid his head down and gazed at the wall. The wallpaper in this dump of an apartment was abominable. Some puke orange interspersed with lightning green over faux gold leaf. It boggled his mind to think that it had been in fashion at some point. He rolled his head just enough to keep Derain in line with his vision, "How long do you think we should wait for them? Got any thoughts on that?"

Derain set the data pad down and intertwined his fingers. His eyes bored into Anton's, but he didn't say a word. Once Rabbit broke eye contact and looked away, he simply stated, "She kept looking for you for three of your years. Don't you think you owe her the same?"

Anton glanced back guiltily, "Yeah." He shrugged his shoulders and took a swig of his drink. "I've never been very good at waiting."

A curl of a smile appeared on Derain's lips, "It's not one of your strong suits." He glanced back down at the screen, "Neither is playing cards."

Anton perked up, "Huh? What do you mean?"

"Those ladies are playing you, my friend." Derain shook his head at the question writ large on the man's face, "Didn't you watch them bet? Each of them knew what the others had while you remained completely oblivious. They played you well."

Anton swore loudly, "Son of a..."

***

"... And were through," announced Luli. "Running final gate communications. System entry granted, no holds." She pulled the visor up to her eyes and keyed through the navigation coordinates for the Erebus system. "And we're locked in for Mithuna. We should arrive in a couple days our time, about a week planet side."

From the comm station, Galena asked, "Should I send an ident request for the Waratah? See if they're out here?"

Jacquie was quiet as she registered a ping from the gate station to the Matilda's hull, "No. Let's keep all outgoing communication silent. We don't know who may be listening in." She slid back into her seat, "Or who may be out there looking for us."

Luli chewed over that for a bit, "Good point. But then that's why you're the Captain and I am but a lowly pilot."

"Shush you," grinned Jacquie. "Lieutenant, grab that deck of cards, would you?"

She opened a small drawer and pulled the cards free. "Should I call for Barney?"

Jacquie and Luli gave a conspiratorial wink to Galena, "He's teaching the ladies downstairs some new tricks."

***

Rosa Keri, the long-time comrade of one Sam Melende, did not like Mithuna. It was a hot and dirty world. Not to mention the humidity. The main activity on this dust ball was to find your drug of choice and take it until you couldn't afford to leave. Why Sam had chosen this backwater to hide out on she couldn't understand. But then, this place was just one stopping point on a trail of many.

Ever since the botched pick up on Chalman's World, their fortunes had only spiraled from bad to worse. Damn that Rabbit anyway. He not only slipped the trap they had set but had gutted their ship in the process. It boggled the mind. What had he said back on the Vogelgesang? She snorted, "Good friends to have indeed."

That was definitely something she

and Sam could use now. Their employers had turned on them after the last fiasco. Most of their allies were either dead or had disappeared years ago. Their only remaining friend, and she used that word lightly, was that bastard, Rabbit. He would disagree. He did have friends and they had disappeared successfully. Until he had shown up again and it was here on this crap mud ball. They knew where he was staying, but no moves had been made on him yet. They couldn't afford to spook him because they needed him badly. He and his friends were their last hope to get out of this situation alive and intact.

The communicator in the apartment rang for an incoming message over the baritone snores of Sam. She strolled over to the comm device and retrieved the grafted message from the jump gate station. She had it set to provide a list of all incoming ships. So far, the one they needed hadn't surfaced.

She quickly scanned through the latest list of ship idents and one caught her eye. The corner of her mouth crinkled upwards. Maybe that tiny glimmer of hope that Sam held fast to had finally arrived. She allowed herself to let hope sweep over her for the first time in a long, long while. She glanced at Sam's sleeping form and decided to keep the news until the morning. Plans had to be set in motion.

***

Jon Gray Lang

Kaplean felt queasy. While it was rarely part of his function as a Captain, interrogation was not new to him. The process would have been more by the book, but Dr. Wyeth had decided at the last minute to oversee the Tiwi clan interrogation. She brought a fanatical touch to the business and Fitzpatrick had taken to it with zeal. He finally understood what had gotten the man noticed by the Special Services branch. He was not only very proficient at the task but took to it as a starving man does to a feast.

The number of Tiwi family members that Dr. Wyeth had the Yeoman retire triggered an immense wave of sadness in him. He knew this was a mostly fruitless endeavor. These people didn't know where their cousin was. Most of them had barely met him, let alone knew a damn thing about him.

At least three generations of the Tiwi's were piled like refuse over the drain in the local law's examination room. Once the Doctor was done, their bodies would be left to rot. The few members left of the clan not interrogated had been born after the man had left the planet.

The only useful information they had retrieved was from one of Derain's brothers. He appeared to be a much older version of the person on the bounty hunter holo ID. Tears had rolled down his face when he told Dr. Wyeth everything he could think of while Fitzpatrick had cut into his grandson.

Jon Gray Lang

He had given up his brother's name and the reasons for his departure. It had been over some spat with their father and his desire to follow in the footsteps of his great grandfather. He had even provided the last date Derain Tiwi had been on Aketi and it had been years ago. The most valuable piece of information he had given up before he had followed his grandson in death was the name of the man's ship. It wasn't much, but at least it was something to work with.

One of the Captain's guards walked up and touched him on the shoulder. He tilted to hear what she whispered into his ear. It was a summons from Lieutenant Hayley. "If you will excuse me, Dr. Wyeth." He didn't bother to wait for a response.

He stepped out of the room and his communication officer looked quite green. He nodded to her as he motioned the two of them away from the door, "Ms. Hayley? What can I do for you?"

The Lieutenant gave a salute, "Sir. We received a hit from one of the gate stations." She held out her data pad, "A ship named the Waratah was impounded under quarantine laws in the Erebus system."

"Quarantine?"

Ms. Shimada spoke up, "That is correct, sir. The gate station personnel listed the ship as having arrived from Leporis gate, a quarantined system." She withered under his stare.

"The, uh, Leporis gate was shut down after the system was declared lost a decade ago from the war." Her hand dropped to her side, "Sir."

Stranger and stranger. The last time they had caught sight of their quarry was when it escaped from one war-torn system. Now to have one of them depart from another war-torn system seemed improbable. Had the two ships separated? "Were there any other vessels listed as coming from that gate, Ms. Shimada?"

"No, sir."

The Captain slowly digested the information. As far as he was concerned, there was nothing left to learn here. Due to time dilation, he knew that the data Ms. Shimada had brought forth would be nearly a month old by the time they arrived on Mithuna. That sealed his decision.

"Lieutenant Hayley, please prepare the ship to be underway within the hour. Set the course for the Erebus system."

"Sir, yes sir!" shouted the Lieutenant, quickly echoed by officer Shimada.

He watched as they beat a hasty retreat back to the space port. He shook his head, turned and headed back into the interrogation room. It was time to tell the Doctor that they were on the move.

twenty-one

twenty-one

Blood & Wine

After their harrowing ride through 'other space', a quiet dinner on the Matilda felt almost outlandish.   The troop commanders struggled to carry on a normal conversation with the crew. Sometimes, the questions they asked were too open-ended and other times, uncomfortably direct. Luli smiled at the effort Jacquie put in to make them feel welcome.

Omega's voice boomed above the rest, "Natural-borns can come from the same birth chamber, yes?"

"Yes, but we call them mothers..." Jacquie answered.

Gamma glanced between Jacquie and Barney, "Does that mean you two are sisters?"

"Um..." Barney murmured.

Jon Gray Lang

Luli stifled her giggles when she saw the look on Jacquie's face. Once she had control of herself, she cleared her throat, "Excuse me, everyone. I need a look-see at our trajectory to Mithuna. Stellar meal again, Galena. Anton has taught you well!" The pilot dropped into a slight bow before she headed out of the lounge.

It was a short walk to the bridge and her fingertips trailed along the worn metal of the bulkhead. Since their attempted mutiny, the level of trust the soldiers gave astounded her. Once the decision was made that Galena was no longer a threat, they treated her the same as everyone else. Luli's lip curled, "Well, maybe with a bit more reverence."

Her booted feet whispered across the empty bridge as she curled up in the pilot's chair. A quick check showed they were still on course so there was little to be concerned about. But something niggled the back of her mind and she couldn't quite put her finger on it. She pulled up the proximity records and had it run through the last couple of hours. Every now and then, a blip would appear on the outer edge of the scan, then disappear.

"Huh. Wonder what that is?"

She selected each occurrence and ran them back to back. Each time, the blip was well within the vicinity of the same point. Her fingers danced across the interface as she ran a triangulation and altered the sensor settings to angle outwards toward that spot. Slowly, the sensors picked up what had been tripping the proximity alert.

She rolled over to the comm and contacted the lounge, "Captain? We've got a shadow."

***

"I think they've seen us, Ms. Basset," Captain Philani moued through the open holo-comm channel.

"A moment, please." Lorin Basset turned to her shipmate, "Winston, come here. The ship's ident proves we've found the runaway." She flipped back to the open comm, "What are our options, Philani?"

He stared down at the diminutive woman as her equally short companion joined her in front of the comm screen. She was attractive in her own way, but incredibly stern. Not that he minded a stern woman. But she was a Titan. He hadn't met many Titans in his travels, yet here he was. These two had hired him to hunt down a third one. And that Titan had last been seen boarding the ship they shadowed.

Titans were a handful. Many people had a tendency to assume that they were weak because of their stature. His own second in command, may his soul rest with Tom, had made that very mistake when they had been hired. Fool that he was, the punishment had been severe but his death quick.   On the positive side, his death had been a good object lesson for the rest of the crew. He sighed.   It also meant that he was the only one left willing to communicate with the pair of them.

Captain Philani gave the woman an appraising look, "There are two options.   We can head further out past their sensor range or we can attack."   He gave a slight shrug, "They know we're out here, so any element of surprise is already lost."

Winston stared out the bow port of the yacht and tried to pinpoint the Matilda in of the sea of black.   His question rang grim, "Thoughts on an attack, Captain?"

Flavio Philani took a report from his latest second in command, Hegge Lynn.   "For a small transport ship, the Matilda has decent armaments, but nothing of great concern.   While her crew is solid, they are few in number.   From the last data dump your agents were able to provide, she only has a cyborg pilot, a bounty hunter, your Titan, and her captain as the crew."   He handed back the report.

Flavio plopped into his seat and straddled the armrest.   He gazed at the two Titans in the holo-comm until they could barely hold their impatience.   With a bravado that he felt was well earned, he answered smoothly, "If the data your spies provided is correct, in a ship to ship fight, we would come out ahead.   But your friend, he might not make it.   Now, if we can board her?   My battle-tested crew of twenty would tear through them like

Jon Gray Lang

a crate of whiskey." His left eyebrow quirked high, "You spent your mazuma well when you chose us. We can capture your Titan friend and with very little risk."

His employers stepped just out of audible range and discussed the options available. At least, that's what Flavio figured. Occasionally, they glanced at him through the holo-comm.

Lorin snarled as she whispered into Winston's ear, "Friend. The androgyne is no friend of ours. It has only made a mockery of our beliefs. Parading about as if it were a male. We do need it alive, though. It must be made into an example to others of its ilk. They must follow doctrine. They will see what happens to those who wish to live beyond the will of the Gods."

"Agreed, Lady Basset," Winston replied. "I don't trust the Captain or crew of that rat-infested pirate ship, but I do think even those miscreants could dispose of the androgyne's companions."

"So, we are in agreement?"

"We are," he said.

Winston Overton gave a small bow to Lorin and stepped back over to the holo-comm. His eyes leveled with the Captain of the Garuda, "Attack them as soon as possible."

Flavio Philani jumped up and danced a jig past the comm, "Excellent choice, my benefactors, excellent choice!" He turned to his second in command and his voice dripped with gleeful menace, "Tell the crew we've got work to do."

***

Jacquie kept an eye on the sensor as the blip grew closer. She gazed out the bow port, but their shadow still couldn't be seen with the naked eye. She glanced back down at the sensor grid and its course deviated back to them. "Luli, hail them please."

"But of course, Captain!" she replied. "Matilda to unknown vessel, please reply with your ident?" She waited a few moments before she triggered the comm again, "Matilda to unknown vessel, please reply with your ident?" After a few minutes of repeating this process, she muttered, "They are not talking."

Jacquie expanded the sensor grid over the other ship. Her lips curled in surprise, "I think they're angling for an attack?" She snorted, "Oh, they are!" Laughter exploded from her.

Galena looked quizzically at the Captain and then over at Luli. Luli just shrugged, while Jacquie kept on giggling until she was red in the face.

"I always feared this day might come. Has my Captain of captains finally snapped?" Luli lamented. "Jacq, are you okay?"

Greater peals of laughter was her only response. With concern stamped across their faces, the two ladies sat there while Jacquie battled to regain her composure.

Luli rebuked her, "Captain, now is not the time for this. They're not going away. What do you want us to do?"

Little noises escaped Jacquie as she tried to control herself. When she finally quelled the giggles that had overwhelmed her, she flipped the comm to the engine room, "Barney, kill the engines and make it look like mechanical failure."

Barney's voice came back over the comm, "Eh? Did you say kill the engines?"

A wicked grin broke across Jacquie's face, "You heard me right, Barney. Kill them and make it look mechanical. Oh! And expect some unwanted company. Lu, adjust our trajectory to make it easier for them to board us."

Luli's face tightened in concern, but she pulled the visor down and adjusted the ship's angle. The Matilda swung out toward the path of the advancing ship. "I've changed it as you requested. Now can you tell me what in the name of the Major you're doing?"

Jacquie stared at the two ladies. She was met with expressions of deep concern for her mental wellbeing. Glee crept past the edges as she crowed, "They've lost and they don't even know it!" Confusion still reigned on her friend's faces. "There is no way they can know we've got a Gods-be-damned army on board!"

Luli started giggling and Galena

slowly joined in.   Soon all three of them were howling loudly.   They almost missed Barney's voice when it came back over the comm, "Okay, she's listing.   Now, will someone tell me what the hell is going on?"

***

On the bridge of the Garuda, Hegge looked up from her console until she caught Flavio's eye, "Hey Captain, take a look at this!"   She pointed to her screen, "Their engine's just died and they're listing into our flight path."

"Really?" he grunted in surprise.   "Ha! Bad day for them; good day for us!"

Hegge bounced readings back off the target ship, "Her defenses just went offline and her heat signature is diminishing.   Flavio?   I think she just lost all power."

A hungry grin lit up Philani's face as he moved back over to the comm.   He threw a querying look to his employers, "From the stories you told me, I was under the impression that this ship was supposed to be formidable in some way?"

Winston   glanced   at   Lorin questioningly until she gave him acquiescence.   He straightened his vest, "Captain, the Garuda is not the first ship we've sent to collect the heathen. We only discovered   its   hulk   months   after   their   last communication, with all aboard dead."

Flavio   beamed   at   the   small   man

before a wheedling grin lit up his face, "And the only rule is that the androgyne, as you call it, lives. The rest of the crew is expendable?"

"Harboring the abomination de Lagnel can only be met with death," Lorin growled. "They chose their fate."

"And the ship and its stores?" asked the Captain.

As she brusquely moved away from the comm, "Do with it as you will. I care not."

Flavio fairly glided back over to Hegge Lynn, "Angle up to connect. No reason to damage our prize. Am I right?"

She beamed back at him as she matched the slow spin of the Matilda.

***

Boris, the leader of the boarding team, settled next to the airlock. At the klaxon bell, the rest of the thieves, cowards, and murderers onboard gathered loosely in front of him. He'd seen some of these bastards kill in the streets. The only thing that had kept him from getting a knife in the back was their fear of him being an even bigger bastard. The decking rocked under his feet as the airlock tunnel completed its connection.

"Alright, you lot!" he yelled. "The Cap says this'll be an easy take. Just keep the dwarf alive! Everyone else is sport. You got that?"

"Keep the dwarf alive and play with

the rest!" shouted one of the butchers in the rabble.

Boris disengaged the first airlock hatch and then the second one. The expanded tunnel lay before him. His magnetic boots clicked loudly when they engaged and he headed down the tunnel to the outer lock of the Matilda.

"She's locked up tighter than a drum. Dalit and Bura, crank this candy shell open. We've got a prize on the other side!"

The two burly fellows ripped the plate that covered the gear housing off and swung the manual crank bar into action. Once the outer hatch was fully opened, Boris strode into the airlock proper and up to the inner hatch. Emergency lights flickered through the hatch window, but the view remained obscured.

"Alright boys, you know the drill. Next verse, same as the first!"

Bura brought the crank forward and Dalit set to it. When the hatch parted wide enough, Boris poked his head in. The ship looked deserted. A mostly empty cargo bay greeted his eyes. From what the Captain had told him, the crew was maybe four or five strong.

He pulled his head back in and nodded at the two men, "Keep cranking."

Once the hatchway was completely open, he faced the riffraff under his nominal command, "Alright, you bloody bastards! Get in there and do what you're good at!" His arm raised and he shouted, "Charge!"

Jon Gray Lang

Suddenly, a shout of "Hold!" echoed from the cargo bay. His men stopped and looked back at him for orders. He strained his eyes and could barely make out a woman with two others across the empty room. "I see the Titan, but neither of them women look like a cyborg. Actually, one of them looks like a worthless drone." His grin grew wider.

The woman in front of the others spoke again, "I offer all of you the chance to surrender. Just know that I hold no love for pirates and this offer will not be made twice."

Boris chuckled and turned to his people, "Keep that one alive for me, lads! Gut the bloody rest!"

With an uproar, the boarding party scurried into the cargo bay. Jacquie and Galena dove to the right and Barney dove to the left.

"Now!" Jacquie screamed at the top of her lungs and the room rattled with the barrage of gunfire.

Boris fell back into the airlock and watched in horror as his mates were decimated before his very eyes. Looking up, he spied a second level crowded with scores of genorgs emptying round after round into his cretins below.

"Retreat!" he roared as he fired up into the balcony.

The remainder of his men ran past him. His weapon clicked on an empty charge as the last man's boots clunked past on his way back down the tunnel. Boris threw the gun in frustration before he noticed all the rifles pointed in his direction.

Jacquie stepped forward and appraised him. She brought her pistol to his temple, "Worthless drones, eh? You should've surrendered."

The shot sent his body tumbling backward into the expanded tunnel.

Jacquie called over to Omega, "We need to take that ship now. Got it?"

Omega replied, "Understood." Genorg soldiers streamed into the tunnel.

"Are you sure this is the best course, Jacq?" asked Barney.

"I gave them a chance," she stonily replied. "I offered them the option of surrender. No pirate has ever done that for me and mine."

Barney sighed as Jacquie hastened into the tunnel followed closely by the Lieutenant. A glance over his shoulder showed him the carnage that decorated the cargo bay. Disappointment masked his movements as he slung his rifle over his shoulder and flagged down some of the genorg soldiers. "We need to get these bodies cleared away as soon as we can."

"What shall we do with them?"

A lead weight sunk into his chest, "Stack them over here for now. We'll space them later."

***

Jon Gray Lang

Galena stayed by the Captain's side as her sisters surged forward. Their mission was to clear the ship of any and all resistance. The pirates hadn't expected retaliation and the first deck fell quickly. A contingent of soldiers had already begun stacking the dead next to the airlock.

Galena grew concerned for Jacquie as they delved deeper into the raider's vessel. Her behavior changed. She rarely blinked and an obsessive eagerness increased with each step.

"Captain, are you all right?"

Jacquie turned on her and her hands shook, "I'm fine! Now keep up or get your ass back to the ship."

Jacquie took off and Galena fell behind. By the time she caught up to her, Jacq was breathing shallowly as she paced next to Omega.

"What's the problem? Why haven't we taken this deck yet?" Jacquie shouted through the bursts of gunshots.

Omega answered back in a flat tone, "The ingress is a bottleneck to the top deck. Their defense is well seated here."

Jacquie glared at the genorg and then at the entryway. She spun around to Galena, grabbed her by the shoulders and growled at her, "Lieutenant. You will clear this corridor. Now. Do you hear me? I don't care how."

Galena weathered the bitterness from the Captain and caught the creep of desperation on the edge of her voice. The Captain's tale of her murdered parents and the abducted Barney sprang to mind. Clarity struck her and Galena's features grew stoic. She snapped out a salute, "Sir. Yes, sir."

Galena sucked in three hard breaths and prayed that no fear showed on her face. She yanked her pistol clear and shouted, "Omega, cover me!"

Her teeth bit down on the knife when she jammed it in her mouth. She leapt out past the corner Omega used for cover and sighted in on the first person she saw. She felt the kick of her sidearm as she fired. A hot burst of pain seared through her shoulder and her pistol tumbled loosely from her hand. It clattered loudly to the decking behind her but she kept moving. She spat her knife into her right hand and dove at the two people hunkered behind a barricade.

Once her body cleared the barricade, her knife went up and into the chest of a man who pushed her away. She flowed with the motion and rolled over a woman who shot at her, but hit the man instead. Galena's knife slipped free of the pirate's ribcage with a wet, sucking sound. She continued the roll and brought the edge of the blade across the woman's throat. Blood spurt out in an arc and the woman dropped her gun in a vain attempt to keep the wound closed. A hand grabbed her shoulder and pulled her back. The raiders slowly bled out in front of Galena.

"Good work Lieutenant," Jacquie growled as she stomped past.

Jon Gray Lang

"Your rush gave us the opening we needed," murmured Omega as she pulled Galena to her feet. "Thank you."

Galena nodded and checked the seriousness of her wound. The genorg soldiers moved further into the hallway and wiped out the handful of pirates that still held their positions. She glanced over at Omega with a question on the tip of her tongue.

"No prisoners," answered the troop commander. "Captain's orders."

Galena nodded in understanding. She and Omega followed the soldiers through the hatch to the third deck. No resistance was found. Shouts of "Clear!" rang out after each room was searched. There was only one hatch left. It went to the bridge.

"Tau-23, get this hatch cut," ordered Omega.

"Sir. Yes, sir." She powered up the cutter on her back. With the assistance of two other soldiers, she began the arduous process of cutting through the plasteel.

**

Captain Flavio Philani couldn't keep his eyes off the shower of sparks as the cutter sliced its way through the hatch. "Only supposed to be four of them! How did they beat my boarding party and my crew? This can't be happening! They can't be taking my ship from me!" It was simply beyond

Jon Gray Lang

his comprehension.

"What are we going to do, Flavio? Do you have a way out of this?" screamed Hegge.

He just sat and stared as the arc completed its circle and a chunk of the hatch fell inward. A woman, who matched the holo provided by the Titan's spies, stepped through the opening. He brought up his gun and sighted down the barrel at her. A pack of the same looking woman followed quickly behind her.

"Genorgs? Genorg soldiers?" he muttered questioningly into the air. "How could they miss that?"

Hegge brought her pistol up and was summarily shot by one of the soldiers. She cried out and collapsed to the decking.

Flavio looked on bemused. How could the Titan's spies have missed this? How could anyone? It was beyond ridiculous. He threw his pistol to the floor and fell to his knees, "I surrender."

The Captain of the Matilda stomped up to him and smashed the butt of her pistol against his temple. As he lost consciousness, all he heard was, "You made your choice, now you get what's coming to you."

***

Jacquie pushed the Captain of the Garuda into the airlock along with his second in command.

Jon Gray Lang

"You know you don't have to do this!" cried out Flavio. He glanced over at Hegge but she was still unconscious. "I'm sure we can work something out. Come on, think about it!"

The airlock closed in his face and Jacquie scowled at him through the airlock window. Slowly, she unlocked the outer airlock and opened it just enough to bleed the air out. She ignored their cries as they begged for mercy. She didn't look away as the air in the chamber evaporated into the midnight of space. After their struggles ceased, she opened the outer hatch all the way. Their bodies tumbled out into space and left no trace in the airlock chamber. She turned and gazed into the stunned eyes of Galena Chadov.

"Now... I think I know how you could make such a harsh decision at Timmony Bay." Jacquie turned back to the hatch window and watched the bodies tumble out of view, "I think I finally understand."

twenty-two

You on the Run

Winston settled into the pilot's lounger onboard their small yacht, the Cyclops. He kept the pleasure craft just out of sensor range of the Garuda. With the flip of a switch, the monitors broadcast the live-time separation of the Matilda and the Garuda.

He crossed his arms and glanced over at Ms. Basset as she completed the laser-comm beam set up to the Garuda, "We are queued up your Holiness."

"Garuda, come in. Garuda, come in." A frown creased Lorin's forehead, "Captain Philani, are you there? My patience wears thin!"

The holo-screen blinked on and she forced a look of calm on herself. "Soon, we will be done with these heathens, Winston. I cannot

Jon Gray Lang

tolerate their presence for much longer."

"Soon, Mother Shepherd, we will be free of them," he muttered.

She waited for the detestable face of Flavio Philani to appear. As the holo image sharpened, a completely different and unexpected face appeared.

"What do you want, Jacq? Wait, who is this?"

The garish privateers had failed. Their prey, the very androgyne that she had hired them to capture, peered back at her.

Rage twisted her face as she snarled at the image, "You! You dare continue to thwart me! By the Gods, I will see you broken on the wheel for the heretic you are!" Lorin's fists slammed against the console when she cut the laser-comm, "The androgyne has escaped my grasp yet again!"

"What are they doing over there?" sputtered Winston.

On the monitor, Lorin caught sight of the bodies as they were jettisoned into space from the Garuda. The corpses glinted like pearls in the night sky.

"Why do the ancestors continue to curse us at every turn!" She jumped to her feet and elbowed Winston in the side in passing.

He glanced up at her and frowned.

"Get us out of here, Winston. I must be free of the sight of the epicene."

With a few quick keystrokes, he

brought up the ship's nav system and set a course for Mithuna. Perhaps they would have better luck there.

***

"Get your troops settled, Omega," stated Lieutenant Chadov from the airlock chamber onboard the recently liberated pirate ship. "Luli will get all of you sequestered for departure."

"There are crew quarters on the second deck of this boat. Should be plenty of room for you all. Hey Galena, keep my ship safe!" Luli grinned as she wrapped her arms around the woman for a brief but tight embrace.

"I have to get back to Jacq for ship prep. Enjoy flying this heap," Galena waved as she stepped into the airlock tunnel.

Alone on the Garuda's bridge, Barney plowed through the ship's diagnostics and made her ready to leave. The plan was to take this boat to Mithuna and claim it as salvage.

He leaned back in his chair and rubbed his brow. It bothered him how quickly Jacq had ordered the raiders executed down to the last one. It so was unlike the little girl he had watched grow up.

He grimaced, "They would've done the same to us."

The comm station lit up with a direct beam connection. He kept at the diagnostic and ignored the alarm. But the alarm was insistent. He slid over and completed the holo-comm connection, "What do you want, Jacq?"

The face on the holo wasn't anyone he recognized, "Wait, who is this?"

The woman's face went livid at the sight of him and dread settled around his heart. What was a Titan doing way out here?

"By the Gods, I will see you broken on the wheel for the heretic you are!" she cursed as she cut the comm.

He stared blankly at the empty holo. As far as he knew, there were only two types of Titans that left the home world. Either, an ambassadorial team sent out for political posturing or a retrieval team dispatched for the capture of illegal runaways. Sometimes, they were one and the same. Queasiness hit the pit of his stomach. She had recognized him. She had known who he was.

"Well, that's done," Luli said as she walked onto the bridge. "We've got a detachment of about fifty soldiers on board with Omega in charge." She hopped into the pilot seat and pulled up the sensor net, "What's that?"

Barney cleared the knot in his throat and murmured, "Another ship was in comm range with the Garuda. I don't think this was a standard pirate raid, Lu. I think they were lying in wait for us."

***

Jon Gray Lang

Perched on the back of the pilot's seat, Jacquie tried to focus through the cacophony of voices that surrounded her on the bridge. In the background, Galena demonstrated to Delta how the nav system worked. At the same time, Luli's report on the Garuda played over the open comm, "At first go over, this junker is in decent enough shape. She should be able to make it to Mithuna without a hitch."

"Oh, by the way," she remarked offhandedly. "Barney caught a transmission from another ship before it bolted and it looks like they might've been in cahoots with the pirates. He doesn't believe this was a random attack. He's pretty sure they were here to take the Matilda. With our more than usual number of run-ins lately, I'm inclined to agree."

"Great," muttered Jacquie. "Any clues as to who they were or what they wanted?"

"They didn't say much, but they were pretty pissed those freebooters failed. We've been tracking them, though. They've been skirting the outer edge of the sensor scan, but it looks like they're heading toward Mithuna."

"Keep them in range, Lu," Jacquie ordered. "Find out everything you can."

"Got it, mon Capitan! Luli out."

Jacquie sat back and drummed her fingers on the armrest.

"Who would lie in wait for us?" asked

Jon Gray Lang

Galena.

Jacquie smirked as she glanced over at the Lieutenant, "Now that's a mighty good question. Let's see," she counted off on her fingers, "We have the Butcher of Timmony Bay on board. Until recently, we had a terrorist, too. Might as well take into account that we also have a small army of what could be considered deserters populating our decks." She glanced over at Delta, "Not that I think you're deserters. Hell, it might even be Derain gunning for us because we left him in that dead system."

"That wasn't on purpose..." Galena replied.

Jacquie commiserated, "I know. To be honest, at this point it could be just about anyone. The better question might be, who doesn't want us dead. We got lucky this last bunch underestimated us. Luck only holds for so long. And as hard as I cross my fingers, I doubt that will happen again."

twenty-three

Don't You Evah

The bridge of the recently acquired Garuda was a hive of inactivity as the ship made its way to the planet Mithuna. Barney's voice droned away in the background while he went over the ship's diagnostics with Omega. Luli strummed absent-mindedly at her ukulele when an audible ding snapped her out of her reverie. Her deep check into the ship's systems had finally completed.

To her consternation, this boat had a newer piloting system. This meant it lacked the direct connect that she would normally jack into. On top of that, the ship's original sensor suite had been torn out and replaced with an apparatus cobbled together from differing manufacturers. While newish, the components had that hastily scratched look of stolen property.

Jon Gray Lang

Luli tapped at her data pad, "Hey Barney, this excuse of a sensor suite sort of talks to its other parts and sort of not."

Barney looked up from his conversation, "It's got issues but it works well enough."

A teasing smile settled on the pilot's lips, "You've got him around your finger, Omega. If there is one thing Ole Barney loves, it's an attentive audience."

"Shush you," rebuked Barney with a laugh.

Luli grinned and went back to her report. The Garuda was a good-sized craft even though she was smaller than the Matilda. She only sported three decks, but her external rigging was designed to carry a couple of standard shipping containers. Fully loaded, the ship would handle like a brick. Empty, she was fast and agile.

Luli flipped back a page, "Have you seen the output on this sublight engine?"

"Crazy stuff, right?" Barney replied. "Whoever did it was either mad, a genius, or both. I still haven't decided."

"A mad genius?" Omega pondered.

Luli laughed, "That's a good guess from what I'm looking at. By the way, how is cleanup going?"

Omega composed herself, "We have made some headway on the interiors but the last owners left a disaster in their wake."

"Too right," Barney groused. "Now if you look here, Omega..."

"Ooh! New star maps!" cried Luli. She set her ukulele aside and copied them to her personal memory. Maybe once the Garuda was put back to rights, her opinion of the ship would change for the better.

A single chime echoed from the pilot's console. The records search had retrieved a match for the yacht from its archives. Luli quickly ran through it, "Well this explains why we've had trouble getting a solid reading off that little sloop."

Barney wandered over and slipped under Luli's arm, "She was finally able to link it? Let me take a gander."

Luli swung away from the station and let Barney have a go at it. His elbow rested on the screen as he scrolled through the report. There was a dearth of information about the owner, not even a name for the vessel.

"They definitely wanted to keep their involvement secret," he murmured. "Standard small yacht configuration from the Jard shipyard. Hmm." He brought up a list of yacht models until he found one that matched its profile. "Enough seating for four with minimal storage capacity. Just a joy rider," he beamed. "Expensive though."

He threw a glance over to Luli, "Tell Jacquie that the ship maxes at four passengers. That should simplify any problems we have with them once we're in port. Well, as long as they don't have any friends planet side."

Luli threw him a sloppy salute and flipped the ship to ship comm over to the Matilda. She relayed the message and received a quick response. "Looks like they have half a day on us. Jacq wants to know if this heap can cut that distance."

An evil grin lit up Barney's face as he waved Omega over to watch what he was about to do, "Now, check this out." He pulled up the sublight engine schematics, "If I tune the input from here to here, it should boost the engine output."

There was a sudden jump in acceleration. At the same time, the Garuda's anti-grav lessened to compensate for the gravitational pull on the ship. "Shouldn't be a problem... no problem at all."

He glanced back to Omega, "Now this is what I was trying to explain to you earlier. It's probably easier if I just have you do it this time..."

Luli monitored the Matilda as it also picked up speed. From her calculations, they would only be a couple of hours behind the yacht once it made planetfall.

***

The two ships touched down on the surface of Mithuna without error. The space port quickly allocated them to different berths, but their almost synchronous arrival kept them close. In fact, the distance between the two was only a short walk.

After Jacquie finished the shut down on the Matilda, she commed over to the Garuda, "Lu? Do you have any contacts in this port? Anyone that might help us track that joy rider down?"

Luli's voice came back, "I might. Let me check into it."

"I'll throw a few fishhooks from my end, too. We need to know who owns her. We can worry about the why of it later. Jacq out."

She glanced over at the genorg commanders who stood at parade rest near the bridge hatch. Her hand rubbed at the tension on her brow, "Ladies? I'm beat. For now, I'm going to ask you and your people to stay on board. We've got a mess to take care of before we can move onto the question of what to do for you and your people. Is that alright?"

Delta and Gamma looked to each other and nodded. Relief hit Jacquie as she slid back into her seat. Her concerns about the soldiers withered away; a problem for another day.

"I appreciate that and thanks for your help back there. The situation might have been avoidable, but there's no such thing as a sure outcome."

"The possibility of victory lies only in the attack, not from the belief in defense," stated Gamma. "We live today because of you, Captain. We follow your lead."

The two ladies excused themselves and passed Lieutenant Chadov as she stepped onto the bridge, "Are you alright, Jacq?"

Jacquie surveyed the hectic space port. Her eyes tracked several ships as they broke their descent for a landing while others launched from the tarmac. The Loader's Union vehicles shuttled along the roads between the grounded ships loaded to bear in a constant, steady flow.

The strain on Jacquie was visible as the twin suns of Mithuna lit the side of her face. "First thing we need to do is find our people. Then we can secure some cargo and leave this rock behind us... and get on with the rest of our lives."

Galena hesitantly placed a hand on Jacquie's shoulder. No matter how new the concept of friendship was, she did consider this woman her friend, "Jacq? I need to know that you're alright. I've never seen you like that before. Like you were back on that ship."

She didn't respond. Her eyes tracked the vapor trails of a ship as it broke atmosphere. Jacquie felt Galena's hand tighten on her shoulder but she resisted the pull to swing her around and face the Lieutenant.

"I need to know, to understand. Is it because of what happened to you and your family? Please explain to me why they had to die."

Jacquie snarled and pulled away, "Leave it alone! You hear me? Just leave it alone."

Galena's hand drifted back while she

studied the woman in front of her. Pain was evident in the compressed wrinkles around her eyes, the tightened shoulders and the way her head thrust forward as if she would have to fight at any moment. A small frown settled on Galena's face as she moved next to her. Together, they watched the spacecraft land and take off.

After some time, Jacquie's demeanor changed. She glanced sidelong at Galena and a wistful smile slowly painted itself across her lips, "When I was little, one of the things I would look the most forward to was our time at the busy space ports. I would sit for hours and watch the different ships take off and land. The sonic booms when they accelerated to break away from the planet's gravity made me giddy."

She gazed at Galena, "Sometimes, I would lie out on the tarmac and wait for the spacecraft to pass directly over me. It was relaxing... almost peaceful. I still find comfort in it."

Jacquie sensed Galena relax as the tension on the bridge finally broke. Her smile deepened. As little as she truly knew about this woman, the truth was that she cared and she was here. Galena was more than a member of the crew, she was part of her family. This small realization gladdened Jacquie in a way she had forgotten she could feel.

As the silence lengthened, Jacquie exhaled noisily and sat up, "Once we get the salvage rights to the Garuda, we'll have to figure out what to do with her."

Galena smiled back, "Any thoughts?"

The grin on Jacquie's face grew a bit wicked, "Well, I don't need another ship. It's hard enough to find work for one boat. So, I was thinking we give it to your sisters. By rights, they more than earned it." A sly look came to her eyes, "There's only one problem with that option, though."

A sad smile broke out on Galena's face, "There is nothing they can own since they aren't considered human."

"Exactly. And that's where you, my friend, come in. How would you like to be the proud owner of a ship, Lieutenant?"

The surprise on Galena's face alone was worth the idea. Jacquie's grin grew bigger as Galena's grew in response and the two of them erupted into laughter.

***

Luli closed out the comm channel to the tower and hung her head in such a way as to stare at Barney upside down, "She's checking the arrival records for us. You sure there was nothing in the direct beam from the yacht that might provide a hint as to who they are?"

"No lass, there wasn't a thing." He glumly looked on, "Nothing except that it was a woman's voice."

"Which I already told her." She rolled around until he was right side up, "Hokay. That's all we got and that's what I gave. Keep your fingers crossed! I'm stepping out to grab a bite," she said as she mimed eating. "Can you believe it? This crappy scow actually has decent snacks! You want anything?"

His head shook in the negative. After she left the bridge, he scurried over to the comm station. He quickly pulled the tower's contact list and scrolled through it until the name, Daniel Faragoi, caught his eye. He opened a comm channel and waited.

"Hello? How may I help you?"

Barney smiled in relief, "Danny boy, it's me. Barney!"

"Barney? The man with unparalleled intelligence? The man of impossible strength? The man with the prettiest eyes ever to be seen?" replied Danny.

"Always the charmer. Glad you remember me."

"How could I forget? You got me this gig." Danny's breath whispered over the open comm for a quiet moment, "It's been over a decade since I last heard from you. How are you guys doing? You still on that rust bucket of a ship, the Matilda?"

Barney bristled, "What do you mean rust bucket?"

"Never mind, I can see she's in port,"

he laughed. "Rare for you to make a social call. So, what can I do for you?"

Barney peeked over his shoulder and made sure he was still the only one on the bridge, "I need some help finding another boat that made port recently. A cabin cruiser; at tops a four-person crew."

Danny's groan came through loud and clear, "We get a ton of those daily. I'm going to need more than that to even begin to start. Is there anything special about this particular one?"

Barney's tone grew furtive, "It's owned by another Titan."

"Oh?" The surprise in Danny's voice was evident. "Family or something?"

"In a way, yes," Barney muttered. "When you find it, can you keep it a secret? I want it to be a surprise."

"Got it. You can count on me."

"Thanks, Danny. I'll owe you one. Barney out."

Barney cut the comm channel and slipped back into the too tall chair. This ship predated the modern auto-fit chairs and his legs dangled uncomfortably. Beyond that and the weird custom job on the sublight engines, in his estimation, she seemed pretty solid. He moved back over to the open diagnostic, closed it and sent it off to the Matilda. From this point on, she was the Captain's concern.

The comm request light flicked on

and blinked at the edge of his peripheral vision. "Danny must've found them faster than he expected," he thrilled. "They must be terrible at hiding." He slogged back over and tripped the comm link, "Garuda is receiving."

"Garuda? I don't know that boat," the voice on the other end said. "Is there a Luli Qing flying it? Last I heard she was still pilot for the Matilda."

Barney got a little defensive, "It's a temp job. Who's asking?"

"Huh? Oh right. Sorry," the voice muttered on the other end. "Can you let her know that Vijay is asking for her?"

Luli popped around the corner with a spoon sticking out of her mouth. Her eyes glowed with excitement when she heard that familiar voice, "Vijay? Vijay Bhatti? Of the illustrious eight?"

"Ha, ha! Lu!" Vijay chuckled over the open comm. "So good to hear your voice! Hate to be the bearer of bad news, though. I'm afraid there's only seven of us now."

Barney stepped away from the comm, "I'll leave you two alone."

Luli set down the bowl of food and plopped herself at the comm station. Barney looked back at her, grinned and shook his head before he left the bridge.

Luli licked the spoon clean and set it on the console, "We lost another one of our distinguished group? Who was it? Which one of us?"

"It was Palba," he said. "Crazy thing is, she was murdered. They pulled her memory core, Lu. I mean they physically ripped it out of her head."

Luli leaned back and just shivered in the chair. "That's awful. Who found her? Was it Jarl?"

Vijay's voice took on a pained tone, "Yeah, it was. And no one has seen him since. He's probably still broken up about it."

"I can imagine." Luli closed her eyes. Palba hadn't been one of her favorite people, but she was one of the old deep spacers and, as Vijay had said, there weren't many of them left. Just seven now. She almost felt worse for Jarl, since those two had partnered up on a ship. They had stuck it out together, even though deep spacers were considered pretty crazy by colonial standards. The corners of her eyes grew moist, but she held in the tears.

"Terrible news, but thanks for keeping me in the know, Vijay. Are you in port for long?"

"Actually, I am," he replied. "I was going to ask if you wanted to do a show together. I've got a gig this week and it would be wonderful to see you."

"It's been pretty hectic of late. I could do with seeing one of the old gang. Count me in, Vijay," she rejoined. "What's the club and do you want to meet up early?"

"The show is in three nights from now at the Club Meltdown. It used to be called the Paradise if you can remember that place."

Luli smiled faintly at an old memory, "I do. I'll see you there then?"

"Yeah. See you in a few. Vijay out."

Luli closed out the comm channel and sat back. Tears spilled against her cheeks. Palba had been murdered for her memory core. Nothing like that had happened in a century or more. Luli dried her eyes, picked up her ukulele where she had left it and began to play quietly to herself on the empty bridge.

***

Kwan Sang knocked on the door to Mr. Leon's office and waited patiently for his call to enter. Her eyes traced the tight grain of the wood when the door swung violently open. Startled, she barely had enough time to move out of the way when a middle-aged man, who reeked of anger, stomped past her and out into the hallway.

As he made his way past, she examined him. There was something familiar about him, but she couldn't quite put her finger on it.

"Ms. Kwan?"

At the summons from the office, she turned and stepped inside. The guard at the door slipped past her into the hallway and closed the door.

"And to what do I owe this visit, Ms. Kwan?" Mr. Leon asked.

She gave the man a small bow from the waist and hurriedly walked over to the desk. She gave her employer a sideways glance, "That man?"

"Should be none of your concern."

"Of course, Mr. Leon. My apologies." She took in a steadying breath and brought out her data pad. "I am to inform you in person when the ship you inquired about has landed at the space port. The Matilda has landed and is berthed in 752-G."

"Excellent. Thank you, Ms. Kwan."

"There's more. The crew names you had me search for arrived in separate vessels." The relevant information popped up on her data pad, "The other ship was the Garuda."

"Oh? How curious," he replied with a lilt in his voice. "That is a known corsair, is it not?"

She scrolled through the history of transgressions logged under the vessel's name, "It would appear so." She looked up at him, "Is this important?"

"Only because I understand that the Garuda is generally for hire by many of our local shipping firms," he grinned. "Information is always important, Ms. Kwan. If not for the moment, then for how it ties into something in the future."

She took that tidbit in and let her

subconscious process it.

"Or in the past," the smile rose up to meet his eyes. "Thank you for bringing this to my attention. That will be all." He went back to his report and pointedly ignored her.

She left the office and mentally reviewed everything that had been said. Information was important, even if you didn't recognize its worth at the time. And that's when it hit her. The gentleman who had brushed past her at the office door was the son of a chairman of one of the large shipping companies. Information was important, indeed.

twenty-four

Eye of Demand

Derain scoured the Waratah's systems in search of any intrusions or bugs. The scan he had run of her interior and exterior had come back clear. But the ship had been tossed at some point during its time in quarantine. A couple items had gone missing, but luck was on his side as they were on the cheap end and easily replaceable. Suddenly, the comm light glowed a cherry red. He glanced over and triggered the channel open.

"Matilda to Waratah, come in Waratah. Matilda to Waratah, come in Waratah."

A smile creased his face, "Matilda, this is Waratah. It is good to hear your voice, Jacq."

The tenseness in Jacquie's voice lessened, "It is good to hear from you, too, Derain. Everything come through on your end?"

Jon Gray Lang

"We lost one of the genorgs back on the station. The others know her designation." He sniffed the air, "And my ship has gained a new scent. How about you?"

"We're all good here. I'll tell Delta that one of the sisters didn't make it." The comm was silent for a moment, "By the way, we've got another ship. Hopefully, it will only be for a little while."

"Another ship? And it just happened to fall into your lap?" he laughed. "You'll have to tell me all about it. Send me your berth number and we'll come by."

Jacquie replied, "My berth is 752-G."

"How opportune, we're only a few down from you."

"Looking forward to seeing you soon then. Matilda out."

He flipped the comm off with a bemused expression on his face. "Another ship, huh? That should be one hell of a story."

***

Jacquie disconnected the comm, sat back and savored a moment of elation. Leaving them high and dry in that dead system had been harrowing. But they were okay; her people had made it. Not only had they all survived, but they were all on the same planet now. Her face lit up as the last of her fears melted away. She couldn't wait to hear how they freed themselves.

The comm blinked as an incoming message made its way to the ship from the port's directory. The sender's ident wasn't one she recognized, but that wasn't a surprise in and of itself. She keyed the comm channel open, "Matilda receiving."

"Oh, how wonderful. I didn't expect to get through so soon."

"Mr. Leon? Is that you?"

"Is that surprise I hear in your voice, Captain Delahaye? But of course, it's me," he replied. "I wanted to thank you and your crew in person for the cargo haul you completed. Would your team be available for brunch, say tomorrow?"

Utterly at a loss for words, she stared blankly at the comm. Her fingers hesitated before she keyed it on, "I believe we can make the time."

"Excellent! I'll have my vehicle swing by and pick you up. Good day to you, Captain."

The channel went quiet and Jacquie sat there stunned. "How did he find us so soon? What kind of trouble did we sign up for?"

***

The awful little apartment they had shared on this dirtball of a planet was a madhouse. Once Rosa had tracked the Matilda to its berth at the space port, she and Sam had set to getting everything packed up and cleared out. She jammed the last item into her bag and tied it closed.

"Are you ready yet?" she called out.

In between a few grunts, he snarled at her, "I will be soon if you would just leave me to it."

Her expression went dark and she left the room to keep her cool. His eyes rolled while he packed up the last few items.

He looked over their collection and it made a paltry sight, "Down to a couple of bags of gear each. Times are tough, but here's to hoping that'll change soon, and for the better."

Rosa waited impatiently until he came out with the two bags strapped across his back. "Let's go," she growled. As they tramped away from their temporary home, she whispered under her breath, "Good riddance."

They made good speed on their way out of the city and down into the space port. Public transport wasn't available out to the ship berths, so they slogged their way in.

The Matilda was exactly where her informant had said it would be. The trawler didn't look like much. But she and her crew had somehow gutted a fresh, off-the-line Special Services gunship and then taken out a highly trained team of ground pounders.

Rosa stopped and whipped around to face Sam, "Are you sure about this?" After he nodded with a scowl, she continued, "They're not going to be happy to see us. Do we have a contingency plan?"

Sam just grunted again and brushed past her and her shoulders tightened in annoyance. On their way to the ship, she broke into a short run to get back in front of him. Old habits still held. She had worked as his bodyguard for so long now that doing something else just didn't enter her mind.

Once they reached the open cargo bay doors, she slowed and put her hand to his chest. He glared down at her hand and brushed it away. As he moved to enter the ship, she strode past him into enemy territory. He glanced up the scratched and dented slab this boat had for a face and followed her in.

***

A few berths over, Anton looked up from the aft end of the Waratah and watched as two of the people he had prayed to never see again waltzed into his home. Incredulous, his eyes widened as he did a double-take. He glanced over at Derain whose indubitable expression could cut cloth. "That the same guy you saw on Chalman's?"

Derain just nodded as his eyes swept the surrounding area, "You go on ahead. This has a bad smell to it." He grabbed Carla and brought her to a standstill, "Ladies? Would you follow me please."

Anton made his way toward the Matilda, albeit furtively. He scanned left and right and thought he saw something out of the corner of his eye. But when he looked again, he wasn't sure.

"Trust in the bounty hunter to have your back," he muttered as he shook his head and stepped onto the cargo bay decking.

***

Galena was busy unstrapping the Rabbit's Folly when she caught sight of two people as they walked into the cargo bay unannounced. There was something about them that struck her as familiar. She called over to the other side of the vehicle, "Hey Jacq, I think you should come around to see this."

Jacquie picked up on the uncertainty in Galena's voice, so she loosened her holster and made sure her pistol was ready. "Coming around now," she called out.

As she stepped past the Folly, she could do nothing but stare at the man who stood before her. She was pretty damn sure it was the same man who had tried to pay her to turn Anton over. She shook her head, "What is it with this system that just screams trouble at every turn?"

While Jacquie came around the front of the Folly, Galena edged slowly toward the back. She picked up the spanner that she had used to loosen the tie downs and widened her stance.

Jacquie stopped about a pace away from the runner and her hand settled on the grip of her pistol, "What are you doing here?"

Rosa looked back and forth between the genorg and the Captain. She set her packs down and raised her hands, "We mean you no harm. In fact, we're hoping you can help us."

"Please! Hear us out," Rosa cried as both women stepped toward them with menace laced in each step. "If you can't or don't want to help us, could you at least give us a listen? Please."

Rosa's eyes grew large when she heard Rabbit's voice behind them as he walked into the cargo bay.

"Well, well, well. Rosa Keri and Sam Melende. What could you possibly want from me and mine?" he asked into the stunned silence.

***

A grim smile spread across Derain's face as seven heavily armed thugs broke cover and headed toward the Matilda.

"I thought so." He turned to the five genorg troops with him, "Ladies? Would you mind assisting me with those fellows?"

***

Anton edged around the two people in the cargo bay. The same two he had once thought of as comrades, but who had only proven themselves to be his enemies. Henon slid into his hand as if it had a mind of its own. His grip tightened on the pistol as he positioned himself in a way that Jacquie and Galena would not be in his line of fire. He knew without needing to look that both Galena and Jacquie were ready for trouble.

Rosa swung around and tried to keep all three of them in her line of sight. She kept one arm raised and gingerly removed the pistol from her waistband with her thumb and forefinger. She tossed it to the decking, "We aren't looking for a fight, Rabbit. We're looking for sanctuary."

His laughter echoed eerily in the cargo bay. "Sanctuary? From me?" He strode toward them as he kept her in view down the sights of his gun, "Weren't you trying to kill me the last time we met? Even after I begged my friends here to free you?"

"There were reasons..." Rosa exclaimed.

"Reasons?" Anton shouted as he slammed the tip of the barrel against her chest.

Sam edged slightly away from both of them and threw a glance toward the open cargo bay doors.

Anton's voice boomed with indignation as he sputtered, "What kind of reasons are there to kill a comrade, Rosa? What kind?" He backed away from her and the confusion in his heart was evident in the heat of his face. "We fought together, you and I. By the Major, you even trained me!" His empty hand cupped his forehead, "Didn't we believe in the same thing? That we could change the future? If not, then what were we fighting for?"

Sam started sniggering. He gaped at Anton and erupted into full-blown laughter. "I can't believe it. You? You didn't have a clue? This whole time?"

Anton glared back at Sam, "Didn't know about what?"

Sam continued to harangue him, "All that work hunting your ass down and you never put the clues together? I always thought you were a halfwit, but seriously? Thank the Gods it won't matter for much longer."

Gunfire erupted outside the hull of the ship and the smile on Sam's visage melted away. He ripped out a pistol hidden in the lining of his coat, grabbed Rosa and shoved her into Anton. A shot rang out in the cargo bay as Rosa stumbled and fell to the decking.

Henon slipped from Anton's fingers and clattered against the decking. His hand went down to his belt line only for him to pull it back and find it covered in blood. He crumpled to his knees in shock. Rosa stared up into his eyes with her hand close to his pistol. He gazed into her eyes and the words fell from his lips, "Please don't..."

Sam shouted with vast relief, "Finally! For years you've been nothing but a Gods-forsaken thorn in my side. Now, I realize you weren't even aware of it. More the fool am I."

As Galena shifted her weight to run at him, he brought his sidearm up and kept it trained

on her, "Ah, ah, ah. You stay there, butcher." He
glared at Rosa, "Get the hell up. We've finally
resolved this fucking problem. We'll be back in their
good graces now."

Pistol in hand, Derain strode into the
cargo bay. Anton's labored breathing echoed in the
chamber as he slowly bled out. Sam stood front and
center with the smoking gun in hand. Without a
second thought, the bounty hunter fired a slug into
the man's back. As the large man tumbled to the
decking, Derain nodded and five genorg soldiers
burst into the cargo bay behind him. They dragged
in the bodies of seven armed assailants and stacked
them against the bulkhead.

Derain strolled over to
Rosa and kept his pistol leveled at her, "Give me one
good reason why I shouldn't."

Rosa stretched out her
arms and legs and lay prone on the deck. She closed
her eyes and prayed.

Derain snorted and
holstered his gun. Jacquie already had Anton on his
back and pressed a filthy rag against the bullet
wound. Galena ran over, kicked Henon away from
Rosa and then kicked her in the side for good
measure.

Jacquie shouted,
"Derain, help me get him in a med tube. You got
the rest of this, Lieutenant?"

Galena's stony eyes
scanned the cargo bay for more signs of trouble.

She pointed at two of the soldiers and then at the cargo bay doors. She waved a third one over to her, "It's under control, Captain. It's under control."

twenty-five

An Honest Mistake

Rosa woke with a shock, only to discover she was strapped to a chair. A chair in the med lab of the very ship she had come to for sanctuary. The Matilda's crew was arrayed in front of her. Out past the plas-glass doors was the largest gathering of genorgs she had ever seen. They stood rank and file in the cargo bay and every last one of them was armed to the teeth. She searched for Anton, but there was no sign of him anywhere. The words ground out past her teeth, "You have interesting friends, Rabbit."

"She's awake," said a voice from behind her. A slap to the back of her head rocked her forward. She shook herself and twisted around as the Captain came face to face with her.

Rosa nodded to her, "Captain."

Jon Gray Lang

Jacquie stood there with her arms crossed. She began to pace in front of the woman, "Ms. Keri. I don't think we've been formally introduced. I know a little something about you and apparently, you know a little something about me."

"I know a little about you, yes," Rosa murmured. She stretched her neck as much as she was able to. "May I ask one simple question? That is before we get down to the interrogation?"

"We ask the questions, lady. Not you."

"Shush, Barney." Jacquie gave her an appraising look, "It depends on the question."

Rosa looked away from Jacquie and whispered, "Is Rabbit still alive?"

"Huh. I was pretty certain you would've asked about your friend. Sam is it?"

"I think you mean was, Jacq," grunted Barney.

Rosa glared defiantly at him, "No. I said who I meant." She twisted around to Captain Delahaye, "Is he alive or not?"

"He lives. No thanks to your dead friend," Jacquie snarled. "Oh, and by the way, we've already found a buyer for your Sam. Seems he was a wanted man."

"Just his head, though," piped up Derain. "That man has a thing for heads."

Rosa grew pale. The rumors in the underworld only spoke of one man who had a propensity to collect the heads of those who had crossed him. She wished Sam were here now just so she could curse him, "Damn the fool!"

She knew she couldn't blame these people. They were just looking out for theirs. The plan had been a gamble from the start. She glanced up at the Captain, "What would you like to know?"

***

Derain left the sickbay after Rosa had rattled off her story. As unbelievable as it sounded, it was difficult not to recognize it as the truth. Or at least what she believed the truth to be. All of the pieces fit into his deductions like a puzzle. He came to a stop in the cargo bay. The genorg soldiers moved away and left him to his work with the eight bodies.

The head of Sam Melende was in a bag next to his corpse. Removing it had been a grizzly task, but mazuma was mazuma and that head alone was worth quite a bit. The other seven had been mere street thugs with no real value. More bother than anything else.

As he took a seat on one of the crates strapped to the decking, he picked up the bag and set it down to his left. Her story had surprised him. The look of shock he wore had been mirrored on everyone else's face, as well.

Rosa said she had joined the revolution all wide-eyed and passionate, firmly convinced that she could make a difference. Pretty much like that dupe, Anton. What robbed her of her convictions had been simple. She quickly learned it was all a farce. The so-called revolution was just a creation of the Consortium. Its true purpose was to track and tag citizens dissatisfied with the status quo and willing to take action against it.

Like many revolutions in the past, the goals of its leaders were erratic and in many cases contradictory. The only thing that tied them together was their anger at the Consortium itself. It was genius, really. The government had figured out that dissension was just a tool to be used for the benefits of the few... the few in charge.

Sam had been the one who introduced her to the truth. Since she already was on the watch lists, she had joined up with him to save her skin. Because of her history as an ex-mercenary, he kept her in charge of training. She trained wave after wave of recruits until there were just too many to control.

The revolution erupted into full swing. Terrorist actions sparked in some systems, while full-blown insurrection exploded in many of the outer systems. The frightened locals clamored for the soldiers to come and quell the rebellion. Their jackboots stomped down many a street while patriotism for the governing body was raised high. And because it was all part of the plan, those who raised a hand to the Consortium were laid low.

The revolution's back was thoroughly

broken when its troop movements and plans were leaked. The media empires broadcast more victories to the populace and the Consortium ground the 'evil' rebels under their boot heels. The kicker was that those secrets had been purposely leaked from the leaders of the rebellion. They were just in the employ of the Consortium itself.

The revolution essentially went home in a box during the police action on Tiburon. All that remained was the need for a top-down cleanup of every person involved who hadn't been in on the ruse. Sam Melende had been a member of the Consortium's elite group, but he had been trapped on Tiburon with Anton. He had assumed, incorrectly, that Rabbit had deduced his duplicity during their time in prison and needed to be silenced. But Anton hadn't figured it out and now he lay in the sickbay with a hole in his gut for his misjudgment.

It sounded like a daft conspiracy theory and yet somehow all the pieces snuggly fit together. Sam's house of cards fell in and he had grown desperate in his search for Rabbit. Desperate enough that he had begun throwing around a name that carries more weight than the Consortium does in some circles. A name that no one took lightly. As no surprise to anyone, except maybe Mr. Melende, Mr. Leon did not approve of his name being used without his consent.

"Your head is worth quite a lot of mazuma, Sam," Derain murmured to the bag. "And

I am very willing to cash in on that."

***

The blinking lights from Doc's chassis lit up a corner of sickbay when Anton woke to a terrible burning in his midsection. His fingers probed the spot where the ache pulsed and he grunted in pain, "Well, that was stupid."

Suddenly a disheveled Jacquie filled his entire view, "Anton? Are you awake?" She took his hand into her own, "Are you in pain? Let me call Doc over."

"No, wait," he whispered. "I want to be clearheaded for a little while." He pleaded wanly, "Please?"

Her gaze shifted from him to Doc until she settled back on the crate she had napped on.

A pained smile blossomed on Anton's face, "What did I miss? Anything important?"

"Oh, nothing much," she said offhandedly before she forced a smile. "We escaped a war zone, then a dead system, took on some pirates, and now we have another ship." She paused for dramatic effect, "Oh, and you got shot."

Anton chuckled until a spasm brought him up hard. It took a bit before he was able to ask, "Another ship, huh? And you're going to give it to me, right?"

"Oh, I already gave it to the

Lieutenant. I like her more than you."

"You always liked the shiny, new crew members best." He grinned as his eyes fluttered closed, "Was this other ship a personal thing?"

Jacquie sat back and gazed at him, with a touch of concern showing, "I took it personal. But none of them are left to take it back, so problem solved."

He grunted in response. "Why the Lieutenant? She's not a pilot."

"Well, it's not really for her. I'm giving it to Delta's folks. They earned that vessel fair and square. But since they can't legally own it, I did the next best thing. It's up to them to either sell it or keep it." She looked out into the cargo bay and spotted Derain standing in the wings. "They were fine with that. Seems they consider themselves all one or something."

"Must be their upbringing."

She laughed a little, "Might be. I'm going to let you sleep, alright?"

"Good idea."

She waited until his face had smoothed before she got up to leave. Just as she opened the door, he mumbled, "Next ship we get is mine, okay?"

A real smile lit up her face as she looked over her shoulder, "We'll talk about it." She stepped out into the cargo bay and the door slid shut behind her. Through the plas-glass, she kept an eye on Anton as he shifted, then relaxed and grew still.

"So close to losing him again," she muttered quietly.

"Jacq?" Derain said into the quiet of the cargo bay. "If you have a moment."

She turned and faced him. Ever since that stupid drunken night of bad decisions, he had stayed on. And not only had he somehow escaped that dead system but now he had waltzed in here and saved the day. It was like he was always there when she needed him and he asked for so little in return. Was it really just to get the Matilda? Or was there something more that he wanted?

"Thanks for keeping him alive, Derain. I can just about count the number of important people in my life on one hand and some are still kicking because of you."

He was a little surprised at her response. She usually kept her feelings tight to her chest when he was around. He had watched her with Anton and it was a far cry from how she dealt with him. Her relationships with Barney and Luli were different as well, but there was still more of an inclusive feel to it. He felt more like an outsider than part of her family. But hadn't he felt the same with his own flesh and blood?

"He's a good fella, actually," he declared. "He's pretty annoying, but he does come through in a pinch. I'm only sorry I didn't get in here soon enough to keep him from getting shot."

Jacquie glanced over her shoulder, "He'll live though, and that's the important part. Now I know you didn't come down here to apologize for saving his life. So what can I do for you?"

She watched as Derain's expression reverted back to his more stoic look and a small pang of disappointment hit her as the door to his emotions closed.

"As you know, I brokered a deal with Mr. Leon concerning our recently beheaded acquaintance. We should earn a tidy profit from it. I happened to mention that we might have another name to deliver, but I wanted to see what you thought about it first."

"Trade in Rosa Keri?" Jacquie brought her fist to her chin and mulled this over, "I think she was sincere in looking for a way out. Let me talk to her first. I'll get back to you on this."

Derain's face clouded and he looked away, "Of course." The bay grew uncomfortable in the long silence before he reversed his gaze, "Barney and some of the genorgs moved the personnel containers to the Garuda. Almost all of them have relocated to that ship, as well." A wry grin broke across his face, "From what I understand, the food stores are better there."

"Some things never change. Armies and their stomachs," she beamed back.

He grew serious, "They are good at what they do, Jacq. Very good. Luli and Barney are working on bringing them up to speed on the Garuda's systems, flight processes, and patterns. And they are picking it up very quickly. Each one that learns the lesson immediately relays it to one of her sisters." Quizzically, he asked, "Are you sure it's a good idea to give them a ship and teach them how to use it?"

"They captured that boat only because I commanded it, and they took it fast." Anger resonated from her and her eyes flashed, "I wanted all of those pirates dead and they made that happen. I put them in harm's way for a vendetta that they had nothing to do with." Her shoulders relaxed, "It belongs to them, Derain. They earned it."

"Okay. A few of them gained my trust on that station, too. I can try to trust the rest."

"Anything else? I need to talk to Rosa before we leave in the morning for our rendezvous."

Derain's mouth slipped into a frown, "I have only one other thing. Word was leaked that Anton was on planet after we landed. The only person I can think of who might have known he was aboard my ship happens to be our host for tomorrow's meeting. Keep that in mind, would you?"

Distaste wrinkled Jacquie's face, "And that's what probably led to Anton getting shot. Got it." She grasped Derain's shoulder and squeezed, "Go get some sleep. Tomorrow is going to be a long day." She watched as he headed toward the lift before her hands clenched into fists, "Trust no one."

***

Rosa rested against one of the walls of the holding cell in the machine room. Her luck had only shifted from bad to absolute shit. The harder she tried to run from it, the smaller and more devastating were the choices she was left with. "Damn that man. I should've expected him to plan something behind my back. Only a fool never learns. Damn me."

"A fool? Who is a fool?" came a woman's voice from the darkness. The Captain of this ship of mystery strode into the dim lighting like an apparition. Rosa kept track of her from the corner of her eye until the woman settled herself onto the crate near the holding cell.

She glared into the Captain's face, "I am the fool for believing that change was possible. I am the fool for believing I could escape the decisions of my past. And I am the fool for misplacing my trust." She tore her eyes away from the woman and stared at the restraints that encircled her wrists. "So, what can this fool do for you, Captain?"

"Hmm, what can you do for me?" Jacquie murmured. "That is a very good question, Rosa. Do you mind if I call you Rosa?"

Rosa made a wry face, "Sure. Why not. You are in control of my destiny so call me what you will."

A dry smile cracked across Jacquie's

face, "Oddly enough, I am here to discuss your destiny, as you put it, with you."

Rosa snorted, "As if I have a choice, Captain."

"Call me Jacquie. I'm sure you have all our names on file." She gave her a querying look, "Would you happen to know where those records might be kept?"

Rosa laughed in response.

"Knowing that you're a government shill, you must know where those records are kept," Jacquie continued.

"Knowledge is power, Captain. And yes we have all your names, your ships' names, and your histories. But none of it is on some file," Rosa said glumly. "Sam didn't trust anyone with it, so he kept everything on his person." She looked down and her hands opened, "I'm sure you've searched his body and recovered all of it."

Jacquie's head tilted as she stared at the woman, "Why should I believe you?"

Rosa's head thumped against the wall of the cell, "I could have easily said there was a secret lair somewhere just to live a little longer and maybe escape my predicament." Her neck twisted as she gazed back into the Captain's eyes, "But I'm tired of running. I just want it to be over... to end." She looked down at her hands, "Do you have any idea how shattering it is to have your beliefs, all of your beliefs, turn out to be a lie? And then have to turn around and use that same lie on others? All in the name of that which you had chosen to stand against in the first place? Just to breathe for another day?"

"In some ways, yes. Yes, I do."

"Rabbit was my last option to keep running and it was thin... paper-thin. But I pinned the last of my hopes on it. Instead, it exploded in front of me like the piss-poor option it was." Rosa's eyes closed and she slumped against the wall of her cage, "Hope is a terrible thing, Captain. Hope is a terrible thing."

Jacquie leaned back against the wall and memories flashed through her mind. Old memories of a time when hope had been strong and alive in her. Hope that had barely withstood the backlash of reality. "Yes it is terrible, but sometimes it's all we have to get us through to the other side."

Sad laughter rang from Rosa as a tear streaked down the lines of her face. The image cut into Jacquie. She had heard that laughter before. She had seen that expression in her own mirror.

Jacquie shook herself, closed her eyes, and spoke, "I will give you a choice, Rosa Keri. Neither option is very good, I'm afraid. We have a warrant for you, but it is from a very dangerous man. We can turn you in or we can release you to your fate out on the streets. You might live for another day or two. The decision is yours to make."

The dry chuckle that escaped Rosa's lips was chilling as if it echoed from the grave. "Then, let my last hour be of value to someone." Her wide eyes bored into Jacquie, "Turn me in for your bounty, Captain Delahaye.   I am tired of running. Let my end be quick."

twenty-six

Gypsies, Tramps and Thieves

The twin suns crested the mountain range and signaled a new day. Jacquie and the crew were up early and milled around the cargo bay ramp. When Mr. Leon's runner pulled up, they kept their eyes peeled for trouble. A dark-suited man and woman with large caliber weapons under their left arms exited the vehicle. The female bodyguard pulled open the rear door on the runner.

The man spoke with deference, "Captain Delahaye? If you and your shipmates would come with us, please?"

Jacquie waved her people forward and slid inside the transport. She was followed closely by Derain, Galena, and Luli. Delta, Gamma, and Omega entered the runner from the left side. Rosa was kept sandwiched between them.

Jon Gray Lang

The woman slid into the front seat and examined the passengers. The door clicked shut behind the driver and the runner slipped onto the road. "Where are the other two? The Titan and the terrorist?" asked the female bodyguard.

"They are keeping an armed watch on my ship," Jacquie answered. "We're on a tight schedule so your other questions can wait."

"Very well." The woman slid shut the armored plas-glass separator and turned to face the road.

The runner slipped through the space port and entered the daily traffic of the city. As far as Jacquie could tell, they were making good time on their way to where Mr. Leon held court on this planet. Well, where this Mr. Leon held court, Jacquie amended. We are legion indeed.

***

Barney watched the runner until it disappeared around a corner. He threw a quick wave to Agnes and she slipped into the driver seat of the Folly. The rest of the team that had flown with the Waratah hopped in after her. She eased the crawler out and slowly pulled onto the street. The Folly's engine roared as it chased after Mr. Leon's vehicle.

Barney crossed his fingers before he flipped the switch to the cargo bay doors. The noise of the giant doors when they clanged shut echoed loudly in the room. He watched as dust eddied around the lights before it settled forlornly on the ground.

"So empty now." His boots clunked in the still air, "Too damn quiet, too." He shook his head as he made his way to sickbay.

The doors slid open at his arrival and he walked over to Anton's med tube. He peered through the window at the sleeping form, "Only you could walk into a room and get shot as soon as you cleared the door. Only you."

He checked the man's vitals and burbled, "Most of the soldiers have moved over to the Garuda so that they can get used to it. Not sure if you noticed or not, but the genorgs you and Derain named really stand out now. Like their names give them something to be proud of."

Barney suddenly chortled, "Color me surprised that it was you who gave them those haircuts! You should've seen the response from their battalion mates! The desire to look different caught on like wildfire. Lucky for us, Galena still sticks out with that brilliant streak of white hair over her scar. It sets her apart. If it weren't for that, we might have trouble finding her in the crowd."

Barney slapped the side of the med tube, "Good talk, lad. I'll let you sleep now."

He walked over and placed his hand on Doc's visual assembly, "Keep one of your eyes on him, would you? Any complications, anything at all and you let me know. Alright?"

Doc's multifaceted eyes glared at him,

"De ko na? Ed to do, che da!"

Barney's laughter rang out as he patted Doc's chassis and left the room. The automaton's curses faded behind him as the door closed. Murmurs from the remaining squad of genorg soldiers drifted through the open hatch of the gym as he rode the lift up. The comm chimed just as he stepped onto the second deck.

A puzzled look hit him as he keyed the comm, "This is the Matilda. What can we do for you?"

"Barney, is that you?"

"Danny?"

"The one and only at your service. I finally found your family's ship. It's pretty funny really. If I had just checked for it under Titan names against the landing date, it would've taken a lot less time..."

"Danny, you're rambling," Barney muttered. "Just tell me where they are."

"Oh... sure," Danny sounded a little cowed. "The ship is in berth 1538-Q. Ship designation is Cyclops."

"Thank you, my friend. Thanks for helping me out." Barney poured on the sweetness, "I haven't seen any family in decades and I can't wait to surprise them."

Earnestness tinged Danny's voice, "I know you're busy and all but do you want to grab a drink with me before you fly off?"

"I can't right now, Danny. Too much

on my plate. Keep yourself out of trouble, will you?" He clicked the comm off before Danny had a chance to reply.

Fear hit him hard. They had found him. Cyclops was a designation that was meant to bring to mind a singular focus. And it was only used by Titan's retrieval teams.

His teeth clenched hard until he forced his jaw to relax. He forced himself to relax and strolled past the genorg troops on his way to the engine room, "Good morning ladies. I just need to grab something real quick."

Once he made it back there, he glanced over his shoulder but the genorgs paid him no mind. He reached down and the well-worn handle on his 'case of trouble' slid into his palm like it belonged there and he headed back out.

As he moved through the gym, he waved one of the soldiers over, "Rho, In case anyone asks, I'm going to step out for a bit. I'll be back soon."

"Understood, Engineer de Lagnel."

"Just call me Barney." He wandered past her and stepped onto the lift.

Rho-11 leaned against the railing on the balcony and watched as the diminutive man left through the cargo bay airlock. A questioning look whispered across her face before she shrugged and walked back into the gym, "The born and their strange ways."

Jon Gray Lang

***

The Matilda's crew were led into Mr. Leon's building. Few guards were posted in an overtly obvious manner, but thanks to the errors from a past visit, Jacquie spotted a few of the low-key ones.

"This way, please," gestured their guide.

She led them directly to the elevators and took them to the fifth floor on a private lift. There was a higher number of guards on this floor and fewer hidden.

They followed her until she stopped and indicated a closed set of doors, "I will leave you here. Thank you and good day." She bowed and headed back to the lift.

Jacquie knocked and a young, well-dressed woman swung the doors open. As she ushered them into the spacious office, she said, "Please come in and make yourselves comfortable."

Jacquie strode right up to Mr. Leon's desk and plopped into a seat across from him. "Lieutenant, get me a drink. Something expensive."

Mr. Leon quirked an eyebrow at her arrogance. He nodded to the Lieutenant as she walked over to his private bar, "The tall, smoky bottle with silver script is what your Captain is requesting." He turned to the woman at the door, "Ms. Kwan? If you please."

Ms. Kwan slowly closed the doors

and joined Mr. Leon behind his expansive desk. A station had been prepared for her and the systems she mainly used were displayed on the screen. She bowed politely to him before she took her seat. But her eyes were drawn to the tall, dark and menacing man who clutched a bulky bag while he paced in the back of the office.

A pair of the genorg soldiers took up positions near the doors while the third brought up a woman bound in restraints.

Mr. Leon addressed to his assistant, "Pay attention, Ms. Kwan. There is an important lesson to be learned here."

Luli strolled over to the windows and let her eyes wander over the sights. "Nice view," she deadpanned. "Your people have good taste in views, Mr. Leon."

"Why thank you, Ms. Qing."

The smile he gave to the Captain as she sipped his very expensive cognac was a little pained. It was a rare vintage that was exceedingly difficult to have shipped from its origin planet. He waited until the Lieutenant fell into parade rest behind her Captain. This, for some reason, made him smile with genuine feeling.

With the occasional tilt of her head, Jacquie had stared at him the whole time. "You are not our Mr. Leon," she said as she took a long pull on her glass. "And this is quite good," she murmured as she set the liquor aside. "So... how is he doing?"

"It is good to see you too, Captain. And with more friends, I see." His palms came together in a quiet clap, "An amazing talent you have to make people trust you... to follow you."

She smiled in return, "It's called being honest. You might try it sometime."

His grin grew bigger. "Perhaps I shall. "Rex, as you named him, was doing well the last time we... communicated." He gave her an odd half nod, "By the way, being given a name was quite an experience for us. A new thrill is such a rare thing and they can be ever so delightful. We thank you for that."

"For another dram of this, you're welcome," she replied as she held up her empty glass.

Derain interrupted, "Can we stick to the business at hand?" He dropped the gunny sack on the desk with a thump, "Per the contract terms we discussed earlier, this contains the head of the man who bandied your name about without your consent."

Mr. Leon's eyes lit up for a moment before he tamped them down, "A Samuel Melende, I believe? The one-time council head of the failed revolution against the Consortium? The very same Consortium that formerly employed him?" His fingers steepled as smugness colored his lips, "That is if I remember correctly. Strange to need a name like mine with access to connections of that sort. Wouldn't you agree, Rosa Keri?"

Jon Gray Lang

Rosa's jarring breath rang loudly in the sudden quiet.

"And you recognize the other we brought in. And I should not be surprised," Derain said.

Mr. Leon's teeth glinted when he turned back to the Captain, "We also have the delivery to the Pequiz system to complete. Ms. Kwan? Please, create separate receipts for the two bounties Mr. Tiwi has delivered and for the cargo delivery completed by Captain Delahaye."

Silence reigned while Ms. Kwan busied herself at her station. Eventually, she printed out the receipts on flimsies and handed one to Derain and one to Jacquie.

"Thank you, Mr. Leon," Jacquie replied with a twinkle in her eye. She slowly emptied the glass and set it down on the edge of the desk.

"The number of people in your employ has grown quite substantially, Captain," he remarked.

"It's crazy the things you can pick up on a planet these days," Derain murmured in the background.

"Oh. Quite." Mr. Leon simpered. "Have you decided what you are going to do now that you have a private army?"

"I can think of a few things," she replied grittily. "But their future is their own. As far as the Consortium is concerned they never escaped that rock."

"Are the rumors true that you have also supplied them with a merchant class ship? Though it is signed over to the Lieutenant."

"That finally got approved? Thanks for the update." Jacquie glanced back at the three soldiers behind her, "The Garuda is all yours, ladies. You can sell it or keep it. It's entirely up to you." She turned back and winked at Mr. Leon as the tiniest of smiles appeared at the corners of her lips.

Delta strode forward and placed her hand on Jacquie's shoulder, "We thank you, Captain." She nodded to Galena, "And we thank you, Lieutenant. We have decided to keep the ship, but we wish to rename it. Would you be able to assist us in this?"

Galena replied, "I will most assuredly help."

Mr. Leon suddenly cut in, "Excuse me for the interruption, if you please. Delta 555-74K, Gamma 768-32Y, and Omega 134-97X? Would you and your sisters be interested in employment? I find that I am in desperate need of people with your particular skill sets."

A frown decorated Delta as she stepped back to confer with her two compatriots. Within a few minutes of deliberation, all three came forward. Delta addressed Jacquie, "Captain? In this situation, what would you recommend?"

Luli turned away from the window and moved next to Derain. "It's all clear out there. Doesn't look like this place is going to be blown up today. So that's a nice change."

Jacquie grinned as she answered Delta, "The pay is great and his people seem to be loyal," she threw a quick nod to Kwan Sang. "But remember, he is still a criminal overlord and that is something you should always keep in mind."

She looked back at Mr. Leon and continued, "He has been known to do underhanded things to the people in his employ, though. Like letting it be known that a wanted revolutionary is in town. Isn't that right, Mr. Leon?"

His eyes glittered and his smile turned rakish, "Such things have been known to happen on occasion. I do hope Mr. Roane is recovering."

"Oh, he's doing fine." Jacquie's face grew dark, "I'll let him know that you asked after him."

Mr. Leon leaned back in his chair with his hands clasped together. "My offer still stands, ladies. But I would understand if you wished to disregard it."

Delta stated into the quiet, "We will think on your offer. May we provide a response within the day?"

"Of course. Please, discuss it with your sisters. May I ask but one question of you before you go?"

Gamma tilted her head to the side, "What is your question?"

"What do you wish to name your freighter?"

Gamma answered immediately, "She would be called the Independence. This would be in celebration of ours."

Mr. Leon clapped his hands, "Wonderful! What a lovely name. A name filled with meaning and menace. Excellent!" He addressed Jacquie, "Is there anything else I can do for you, Captain?"

Jacquie had watched Mr. Leon's eyes during the entire conversation and his gaze had fallen on the Lieutenant quite a few times. More so than on anyone else. She straightened up and pushed the glass slowly away from her, "I have only one question for you." She stared at him before she slowly eyed Galena, "Are you surprised to see her? Standing? Alive?"

"Oh, no, Captain. I am quite pleased to see the Butcher of Timmony Bay standing before me." His hands laid flat on the desk, "You see, I am a bit of a fan. I have enjoyed the tales of her exploits."

Ms. Kwan felt a sudden change in the room. She shied away from the tenseness that emanated from Mr. Leon and the ruffians on the other side of his desk. Her eyes darted back and forth as some sort of altercation built right in front of her and she hadn't a clue why.

"Really? Could you tell me why you had her injected with this?" Jacquie growled as she slapped a small vial filled with blue dust on his desk.

His movements were too fast to track.

In the blink of an eye, he had leapt over his desk, dragged Jacquie bodily from her chair and slammed her to the floor. The veneer of self-control slipped from his face as he pressed a knife against her throat. All of this happened before anyone could react.

His eyes narrowed as he spoke into the shocked room, "Laying accusations is a dangerous hobby, Captain. I would not recommend making it a habit."

Jacquie's eyes were wide as she sucked in breath after breath in quick succession. Slowly, the presence of the knife left her throat and Mr. Leon's demeanor changed back to the oddly polite businessman. He reached down, helped her to stand and dusted off her shoulders. As he stepped back to his desk, he dropped the knife into the Lieutenant's lap.

"I would say that we are done," Jacquie stuttered as she motioned for the door. "Thank you for the business, Mr. Leon."

"I do hope this small altercation won't prevent us from working together in the future," he offered to her retreating back. The rest of the group followed her lead and only Galena looked back. She slid the knife home on the inside of her belt.

Once Jacquie crested the door, she heard Mr. Leon say with an undertone of anger, "Ms. Kwan? Please request a direct communication with the Copperhead at their earliest convenience.

Jon Gray Lang

There are questions I need answers to." Her shoulders relaxed a little as she pondered that piece of information. Mr. Leon was not infallible.

After they left the office and the door had swung shut behind them, Kwan Sang worked on getting a direct beam communication to the jump gate for the Copperhead. Her eyes remained averted as Mr. Leon opened the sodden bag and removed Samuel Melende's head. With careful hands, he placed it on the corner of his desk. Halfheartedly, the woman left in restraints watched him.

"Now what should I do with you, Rosa Keri?" he asked.

She glumly stared at Sam's head while his dead eyes gazed emptily back at her.

Mr. Leon leered as he moved toward her. He released the bonds that held her wrists together and lifted her face to meet his eyes. "You do have a great many skills, Ms. Keri, do you not? And your life is mine to do with as I please." He shook her, "Is this understood?"

Her nod of acquiescence was limp and devoid of spirit.

He grumbled a bit as he straightened her collar. "Now... how would you like a job?"

twenty-seven

Life's Been Good

The trip back to the Matilda in the Rabbit's Folly was uneventful. Not a single shot was fired nor was a single blow lobbed in their general direction. After the heated end to the meeting, it made for an oddly peaceful ride through the city.

Once they arrived back at the ship, the Captain helped the genorg soldiers tie down the Rabbit's Folly. She waved goodbye to the last of them as they headed off to their newly christened ship, the Independence.

"Do you think they'll take the deal?" asked Jacquie. "I know they'll let the others have a say."

"They'll take it," stated Galena.

"You sure?"

Galena's lips pursed into a sad smile,

Jon Gray Lang

"Old lessons are hard to unlearn, Jacquie. A genorg without a job is considered defunct. They'll take it. I'm going to say my goodbyes. See you later."

Galena followed her sisters out of the ship and Jacquie was left to her own devices in the silent cargo bay. It was with a pang that she realized the ship was going to feel empty without them.

She went to check on Anton. The man was eager to get out of the sickbay and pleaded for some form of duty.

"I'll think about it," she muttered as she shut the plas-glass doors behind her.

Luli had gone up to the lounge to practice for the upcoming show while Derain had flown off in search of any open warrants. This reminded Jacquie that she needed to find cargo so they could leave the planet and get on with the rest of their lives.

Although they were pretty flush with the recent payments, she knew the currency wouldn't last. The docking fees alone were gouging a growing hole in their budget, but everything was surprisingly normal for a change. She hardly knew what to do with herself.

Jacquie made her way to the bridge to get a line on their next shipment. As she got off the lift, she heard Luli chatting away with someone. Their conversation was punctuated with laughter and music. She hunkered down at the comm station and sported a wry smile, "Let's see where people want their cargo sent."

***

Galena had gotten used to having her sisters underfoot and watching them leave had been harder than she had expected. They had brought back memories of her days in the training pod when she was little. But she also found a great sense of joy in the knowledge that they too would get to choose their own future. The experience was exceedingly rare for genorgs and she gloried in it.

A tiny smile traced its way across her lips as she walked across the empty bay toward the med lab. Anton's curses could be heard before she entered and Doc's responses bleated loudly once the doors opened.

"Still not allowed to leave, I see," she said as she took a seat next to Rabbit's open med tube.

With a silly grin pasted across his face, he replied, "Afternoon Lieutenant. How are you doing on this fine day?"

Her eyes lit up, "You're awfully chipper this morning. Could you let me in on the secret?"

"Oh, it's no secret." His grin grew larger. "Now that we know for sure it was Sam who was after us, and he is no more, we are free and clear. I, for one, could use a little less excitement in my life for a while," he pointed to his bandages.

"Do you think you can handle it? I

find it hard to believe that a man nicknamed the Rabbit would crave less than constant excitement."

"You would think so, right? But I've had enough to last me for a very long time." His left brow shot up, "By the way, have you seen Barney? I had some ideas for the Waratah and wanted to run it by him to see if they're even worth doing."

"No, I haven't seen him. Rho-11 said that he had gone out earlier this morning to take care of some task."

"Oh good, good." A crafty expression flitted across his face, "Have you ever played poker, Lieutenant?"

***

Barney laid out flat on the top of a small hillock that overlooked the berth of the Cyclops. He had staked out the ship since early morning, and the only activity had been that of a male Titan who left the ship and returned a half-hour later. No one else had come near the vessel.

The personal yacht was a garish red popular with the priesthood of Titan. Her lines were very much the standard of the shipyard where she had been constructed, which meant she stuck out like a sore thumb. Amongst the many ships in the surrounding berths, she was an oddly supine craft. Smaller than the Waratah by about four meters and left little room for much else besides the seating for four. Unlike the Waratah, she should have an internal atmosphere. The little boat would have some offensive capacity, but that was dependent on the craft's purpose.

It had been a long time since he had last seen a retrieval vessel and the sight of this one on the tarmac depressed him. Travel outside of the home system was publicly frowned upon and yet there it sat. Normally, they carried a crew of at least two, but they had left Oros to capture him in particular.

"How long have you been searching for me?"

He squinted against the glare from the twin suns as he kept watch on the ship for any movement. As if on call, a female Titan exited the craft and stood there. His eye dropped to the scope on his rifle and he sighted in on her. The hated priest robes hung loosely on the woman who had cursed him and his mind took an ugly turn.

"One shot and you're gone," he whispered. "One shot and whoever else is on that boat will come out; then my problems will be solved."

"One shot," a male voice mocked from behind him.

The blunt end of a silencer pressed into the back of his neck. Barney opened his hands and spread them out from his body and away from the rifle. His head smacked against the ground when his hands were jerked behind him and restraints clapped around his wrists. A vicious kick struck him in the ribs and he struggled for breath.

"Come on. Get up," said the voice behind him and another violent jab slammed into his side.

Barney slowly got to his feet, "Where are we going?"

"You? Why you're going home, Titan. You're going home."

***

It was late in the evening on board the Matilda and the lights were turned down low. The only occupant in the mostly empty lounge was Luli and she had just run through a song that Vijay had sent her. The thump of Jacquie's boots echoed down the hall before she stomped in, her face flushed with anger.

"What's got you in a tither, Jacq?"

"I can't get a shipping agreement for a cargo haul and they all say the same thing."

Luli shifted and gave her some room on the couch. Jacquie plopped down next to her.

"What do you mean?" asked Luli.

"It would all go smoothly until I mentioned the Matilda." Her hands rolled into fists, "Then there would be excuses or they had an agreement with another ship and the comm line would go dead."

"Did we get blacklisted or something?" Luli pondered, "Who would want us blacklisted?"

"I don't know, but I'll find out. And when I do, those who are responsible will regret it."

Galena's head poked into the lounge, "Oh! Hey, have either of you seen Barney? Or heard from him recently?"

Luli checked the time, "He's still not back?"

"It's gotten pretty late," Jacquie muttered. "Does anyone know where he went?"

Both Luli and Galena shook their heads in the negative. Jacquie's brow furrowed, "Luli, can you check the comm logs?"

"Sure thing, Jacq." Luli said. "I'll be back in a little bit."

Galena moved out of the way and Luli slipped by. She returned a few minutes later.

"Only one comm on file from earlier today and it was for Barney. He spoke with Daniel Faragoi."

"Danny? I remember him. Didn't they date for a stretch?"

"I think so," answered Luli.

"That reminds me," Jacquie replied. "Did your contact get back to you about that ship? Mine retired a few years back."

Luli responded, "Yes, but she's been transferred to one of the station satellites and most of her system IDs are still locked. Let me see if I can get a hold of Danny and find out what they talked about."

"Let me know as soon as you know, okay?" Jacquie stood up and headed for the hallway, "I'm going to track down whoever blacklisted my ship."

Luli followed her out of the lounge. Jacquie rode the lift down a deck, hopped out and keyed the latch to her cabin. Once the hatch closed, she kicked her comm on and requested a connection. In time, a well-dressed Mr. Leon appeared on her screen.

"Ms. Delahaye. So wonderful to hear from you again."

Jacquie growled, "Did you have us blacklisted? Was it you?"

"Blacklisted? Why no..."

Jacquie interrupted him, "You did, didn't you. What kind of a game are you playing? This is my livelihood..."

Mr. Leon's face tightened, "Hold on! Now hold on, Captain. I did not get you blacklisted. Do you understand? I would have no need to do such a thing. I may have a lead on who did, though."

That made her stop. She regained her composure, "You've got my attention."

"Wonderful," he replied. "Now, remember that ship you took in for salvage on your arrival? Her crew was known to be in the employ of many of the conglomerate shipping companies in this system. Most of what comes and goes through this system's jump gate is controlled by them and you removed one of their not-so-secret weapons against their competitors. You've gone and upset their apple cart and they're displeased."

"That is quite a lead you have there, Mr. Leon. Would I be mistaken in believing that you own some part of these conglomerates?"

He took a breath as he smiled at her ingratiatingly, "I was approached earlier this week to take you and your ship out of their equation, but I turned down the offer. I feel that I owe you a debt, so I've put the word out to dissuade anyone else from taking the job."

"Well thank you for that," she muttered. "Screwed if you do, screwed if you don't. Leaving this system empty is going to hurt."

"I am willing to work out a cargo offer to patch up any bad blood that may flow between us, Captain. I have thoroughly enjoyed our good working relationship and would like it to continue." He glanced at something off-screen, "In fact, I have some cargo I need shipped off-planet by the end of this week."

"Well, it's your lucky day," she grumbled. "You've got me over a barrel. I need the work and no one else is hiring."

"Excellent!" clapped Mr. Leon. "I will have Ms. Kwan whip up an agreement and get it out to you by the morning." His tone became conspiratorial, "The memory of the conglomerates is short and you should have no trouble finding work here by next year. If there is nothing else? Then, goodnight to you, Captain."

Jon Gray Lang

"Goodnight, Mr. Leon." Jacquie cut the comm and flopped back onto her bunk. "Just when it all becomes clear, the waters have to get all murky again. Fingers crossed it's only one delivery and then back to normal."

The comm lit up and Luli's voice came through. "Jacq? You there?"

"I'm here, Lu. You get hold of Faragoi?"

"I did. He said Barney asked him to look into a ship that landed out here recently... said that members of his family were on board." Luli's voice had a questioning tone, "Is that possible?"

Jacquie threw her arm over her face and exhaled loudly. "It could be. If he's not back by tomorrow morning, we'll worry about it then. Jacquie out."

***

Winston returned with the news that their departure had been delayed until late in the evening on the following day. Lorin Basset struggled to keep the anger in, "We're stuck on this planet for another cycle."

Their prize lay tied up in the back of the ship and the ugly thing's beady eyes watched her every move. Her anger only increased, "Look away demon or I'll carve out your eyes!"

With a grimace, Barney looked away. The news that their departure wasn't until tomorrow night had given him some hope. More time meant more chances to escape. If that was even possible.

The yacht's layout was a minimalist's dream. The bow of the craft was taken up by the primary console and two seats. A large comm screen filled out the port side and the aft housed a small kitchenette. Removable paneling covered the walls which, he assumed, gave access to the physical systems of the ship.

The straight-backed woman paced back and forth in the small open space while the male Titan dealt with a large man at the airlock hatch. The same man who had brought him down here.

"They're a tight-knit bunch. There may be more trouble in the coming day," Winston stated. "We will pay you and your underlings for your time."

The hired thug gave a quick nod before he opened a comm channel, "We've another day on the books, boys. Stay in position and be on the looksie."

Barney swore he heard two replies before he received a kick in the ribs from the priestess, "Mind your business, androgyne."

His 'case of trouble' was so close. It leaned lopsidedly against the bulkhead near the airlock. If it had been a foot closer, he could've been free in moments and his problems solved.

"Where's that bastard Rabbit when you need him?" he cursed quietly. Time was

Jon Gray Lang

counting down and he still didn't have a plan.

***

Despite the cocktail of pain killers that coursed through his system, Anton had gotten up and prepared breakfast. The clatter from the galley was intermixed with his humming when Jacquie walked in.

"Can't keep you still, can I?" Jacquie groused as she grabbed a plate and headed over to the table.

Anton grinned at her, "Can't keep a good man down, I hear."

"When you find one, let me know," she joked back. "Anyone seen Barney this morning?"

"He hasn't returned," answered Galena between mouthfuls.

"Still? Well, he's an adult," muttered Jacquie. "I'm going to need you both to stay close to the ship. I signed off on Mr. Leon's shipping contract and it includes a couple of the big freight boxes."

"Some boring honest work? I'll take that," Anton announced.

The comm chimed and then chimed again. "That's probably the first drop off," Jacquie sighed as she looked down at her uneaten breakfast.

"I'll take care of it," Galena announced as she headed for the lift.

The rest of the cargo arrived piecemeal throughout the day. The three of them kept busy as they stowed the smaller crates and got the first of the containers clipped on.

The Waratah returned about mid-afternoon. Jacquie watched as the ship flew over the back of the Matilda and disappeared into the hangar.

Anton wiped the sweat from his brow and said, "Galena and I can get this last freight box locked down, Jacq."

"You sure?" she asked.

He waved her away, "Go ahead and see if he's heard anything."

It was a short trip to the hangar. She caught up to Derain just as he yanked the last tie-down tight to the decking.

"Nice form. That'll keep her from slipping," she smiled. "You hear anything from Barney?"

Derain wiped the grime on his hands against his pant legs, "No, not me personally. He still hasn't shown up?" Concern colored his response, "That's unlike him. You've known the man longer, should we be worried?"

"I don't know," she replied as she hit the switch to shut the hangar bay doors. The light from the outside world narrowed to a ribbon until it completely disappeared. "I just don't know."

***

Luli was deep in the closet in her cabin when the comm chimed, "Lu? You there?"

She shut the closet door and responded, "Lu here. What do you need, Jacq?"

"Barney still isn't back. Did Faragoi say anything else?"

"He's still not back? That's not like him at all." She went back over the conversation, "To be honest, nothing sticks out."

"I'm heading over to the Garuda... I mean Independence. I'm going to find out exactly what he said to Rho."

"I'll comm Danny and double-check on what Barney said to him. Luli out."

***

Jacquie stepped off the decking of the Matilda and out onto the tarmac. With Galena and Derain in tow, she headed for the berth of the Independence. Once it was in view, she picked up speed.

The hull of the Independence had been scrubbed clean. The rust spots had been sanded out and primed. Jacquie gave an appreciative nod to the work as she made her way around the vessel. She didn't have any cargo bay doors on her, only an airlock. This fit with her design since she didn't have a large cargo bay. She had been constructed primarily as a container transport ship.

When the three of them walked to

the open airlock, Jacquie called out, "Ho, Delta. Permission to come aboard?"

One of the genorg soldiers stepped forward, wiping dirt from her hands with a filthy rag, "Of course, Captain." She stuffed the rag into a back pocket. "The Lieutenant and the hunter are welcome aboard as well. Would you like me get Delta for you?"

Jacquie entered the small cargo area of the ship, "Actually I came to talk to Rho-11. Would she be available?"

"Rho-11? Yes, I believe she is. Please wait while I retrieve her." The genorg gave a slight bow and disappeared into a passageway in the ship.

Jacquie wandered around and appraised the cargo area. She glanced over her shoulder at Galena who also performed her own inspection. Derain leaned against a section of bulkhead with his arms crossed.

"She's in much better shape than the last time I saw her," Jacquie commented. "Your sisters have been working hard, haven't they?"

Galena just gave a strange half-smile, "Of course, Captain. A genorg with no function is soon retired. So we always find something to do."

Derain laughed sharply at this.

The wait for Rho-11 was short. She and the genorg who had let them on board walked into the room, followed by Gamma.

"You asked for me, Captain?"

"Yes, Rho. It's about my engineer,

Barney," began Jacquie. "You were the last person to speak with him before he left. Can you tell me exactly what he said to you?"

"Exactly?" Rho-11 deliberated a moment, "He said that he was going to step out for a bit, but would be back soon." Her head tilted slightly, "Is he not back yet?"

Jacquie muttered in frustration, "No, he isn't. Was there anything strange about his behavior? Did he take anything with him?"

"I do not know him well enough to know what would be considered strange behavior, Captain." Her eyes traveled along the ceiling of the bay, "He did take a long wooden box with him, though."

Derain interjected, "His 'case of trouble'? That's a bad sign, Jacq."

She cursed. "It most certainly is. Gamma, can we use your comm? I need to check in with my ship."

"Of course, Captain. Follow me." Gamma led the way as Rho-11 bowed slightly and returned to her task.

Once they were on the bridge, Jacquie commed over to the Matilda, but there was no response. "Come on, damn it!"

Luli's voice came through suddenly, "This is the Matilda. Is that you cursing us, Captain?"

"It is. What did you get from Faragoi?"

"I'm chatting with him right now." Dead air filled the comm channel before she replied, "Is it bad?"

"Could be," Jacquie groused. "I'm hoping he remembers some detail that would be useful."

Luli commed back, "I just remembered something. Barney mentioned a direct beam communication from that yacht we followed in. There should be a record of it."

"I'll look into it. You tell me immediately if Faragoi remembers more. Jacq out."

"I'll comm right back. Luli out."

Jacquie flipped through the comm logs until she found the archive records. It took a while to get through the long list and access the most recent entries. Luckily, there was only a handful just before the ship made planetfall. She chose one of the more recent entries at random. A small woman appeared on the screen and Barney's voice faintly crackled over the comm speaker.

Derain leaned over Jacquie's shoulder, "Is that a Titan?"

Jacquie watched in dread as a litany of curses poured out of the woman on the holo. The bridge grew quiet as the woman's voice screamed, "By the Gods, I will see you broken on the wheel for the heretic you are!"

"Family, huh?" Derain coldly remarked.

Jacquie scrolled through the other

archived messages and selected the previous one. The same woman appeared on the screen and the recorded voice of the late Captain of the Garuda played through, "Harboring the abomination de Lagnel can only be met with death," rang out in the silence.

Jacquie felt sick. Fear for her friend struck her. She felt Derain's hand go to her shoulder to steady her. This was bad. It was worse than she had imagined. Barney had offhandedly mentioned retrieval teams before. She sucked in a breath and blew it out slowly.

The comm chimed and Luli's voice came through, "Jacq, you there?"

Jacquie closed her eyes and commed back, "Go ahead, Lu. I'm here."

The worry in Luli's voice came through loud and clear, "It's bad, isn't it?"

"Did Faragoi give you anything? I need to know," she muttered in a cold voice.

Luli's tone calmed. "Barney had asked for the berth number of a ship that had arrived before us. The joy rider's at 1538-Q. There's a problem though."

"Great," Jacquie spat out of the corner of her mouth. "What's the problem, Lu?"

"The ship in that berth is cleared for takeoff in about three hours."

Jacquie's gaze slid to Derain, "Then we still have some time."

"I'm going to cancel the show and be

right there."

Jacquie keyed back, "No, Luli. You make that show. It's been too long since you've spent any time with another deep spacer. In fact, take Anton with you. He must be going stir crazy by now."

"This is more important, Jacq," Luli rejoined.

"It's not that bad, Lu. We're just going to meet Barney and pick him up, that's all."

"You sure? You don't sound sure," Luli persisted.

Derain keyed the comm, "It's not a big deal. We've got it under control. Enjoy the night." He made cutoff motions to Jacquie.

Jacquie took the comm, "Say hi to Vijay for me and play a good show for Anton. He needs it. Independence out." Jacquie pinched the bridge of her nose and frowned in concentration. "Can we borrow some of your people, Gamma?"

"Of course, Captain. I will call for volunteers now." Gamma threw a sharp salute and then left the bridge.

Jon Gray Lang

twenty-eight

Gaily the Troubadour

"Anton, you ready to go?" Luli yelled into the med lab.

"Almost! I'll need a few minutes to get my crap together."

"I'll be in the crawler," Luli said as she slipped into the driver's seat.

A moment later Anton threw his coat in the back and hopped in through the passenger door. "Finally free of the lab," he exclaimed. "Finally! Doc thinks I'll live and I get to hit the town. Can you believe it?"

Luli looked preoccupied as she pulled the crawler out of the ship and drove through the space port. Something was on her mind and he didn't want to intrude. But once they were out on the main streets, Anton couldn't take the silence any longer.

"Luli, what's going on?" he asked. "Where is everyone else? Are we meeting up at the club?"

"They'll be coming later. They had to go pick up Barney first." A side glance showed the concern etched into his face. "Uh, do you want to hear a song I'm working on?"

"Barney's still not back?"

"I already said they're swinging over to pick him up tonight! Do you want to hear my new song or not?"

The vehemence in her voice took him back, "Um sure, Lu. You know I love to hear you sing."

"Well now I don't want to," Luli pouted. "Thanks for ruining the mood."

Anton relaxed as he laughed, "Now you're just playing with me."

She threw him a quick grin as she took a left onto the main street of the port city. "I'm just nervous. I haven't seen Vijay in years."

Anton asked, "Have I met Vijay? Wait, he's the drummer, right?"

"Good memory! Whoever said that block of meat in your head is a placeholder was so wrong," Luli quipped. "You met him about a year before you left us. In ship time, of course."

"Of course," Anton responded. "How's he doing? Is he still flying with the same crew? What was his old boat called?"

"The Diaskorpizo. He doesn't fly with them anymore. Now he works for a local conglomerate. Just short in-system jaunts." She replied wistfully, "I think he's finally settled here."

"Is that something you want to do, Lu? Settle down on some rock?"

"It's crossed my mind sometimes, but then I would miss you guys!" She slapped him on the shoulder. "Anyway, Vijay just made this place his home after Palba died."

"Palba? Palba Lazano?" Anton asked, incredulously. "One of you deep spacers dies and it's not huge news? How is this the first I'm hearing of it?"

Luli grew quiet, "Someone murdered her, Anton. And, from the little that Vijay was able to tell me, the person or persons who did it just left her body in some alley after they pulled her memory core. Like she was trash."

Anton sat back and gave her shoulder a light squeeze. Someone had murdered one of the legendary deep spacers and gotten away with it was proof positive that the systems were less safe. And did the Consortium do anything about it? No. All they cared about was controlling the trade between the systems.

"Wow, that must've been hard to hear, Lu. I can see why you're so nervous." He patted her knee, "How about we lighten the mood and sing an old ditty."

She goggled at him, "But your voice is

horrendous."

Anton growled in mock outrage, "It is not!"

Luli giggled as she said, "Did you have anything in mind?"

Anton inhaled and let loose with, "Gaily the troubadour touched her guitar..."

Luli's laughter rang out as he jumped into the next verse, "When she was hast'ning home from the war..."

The Folly flew around the corner with the two of them singing at the top of their lungs. Luli brought the vehicle to a stop where the light from the sign for Club Meltdown splashed across the windshield. All the while, "Lady love, lady love, welcome me home!" rang from inside the crawler.

***

Galena dropped to a knee and peered around the back end of a trawler. After a quick search for movement around the small reddish ship in the distance, she signaled the rest of the team to come up behind her. Once Agnes and Alice arrived, she pointed to her eyes and waved them forward. They fanned out and cut to the right. Rho-11, followed shortly by Daphne, came up behind her next. She had them fan out to the left.

Jacquie and Derain arrived moments later, followed quietly by Anne and Carla. The

Lieutenant motioned them all to the ground. Anne nodded at the nonverbal directions and broke off to the left while Carla broke off to the right.

Galena kept an eye on the boat as she whispered to the Captain, "You would think they would have some guards posted outside, but it looks clear."

Derain grunted, "I'm not a strong believer in the obvious."

Galena's face lit up with a grim smile, "Me either. Do you want to be the one to flush them out?"

A low chuckle was Derain's only response.

Jacquie spoke up, "I'll do it. He's my crew, so he's my responsibility."

Derain grew quiet and hunkered against the ship. Galena nodded and signaled the Captain move forward. "Be careful, Jacq."

"No hitches, please. Let this go smoothly," Derain prayed as Jacquie got up and slipped off toward the little ship.

277

twenty-nine

Stuck in the Middle

The Paradise had gone through some serious remodeling after it had been renamed Club Meltdown. Gone were the gaudy underwater scenes painted on the walls, the temple ruins theme, and the merfolk outfits for the staff. Now it was all bright orange and red, with smoke wafting through the air. The walls dripped and pattered onto a floor that flowed like magma underfoot. The poor staff was now obliged to wear uniforms that looked like it was on fire or in the process of slowly melting off of their bodies.

The club was packed. It was wall to wall patrons while they waited for the show to start. The crowd knew tonight was a special night. It would be a once in a lifetime show with not one, but two deep spacers on the same stage. And once word

Jon Gray Lang

had spread, tickets had quickly sold out to maximum capacity. However, the club looked like it planned to oversell tickets as the line out the doors wrapped around the corner and continued to grow in length.

Luli led Anton backstage and deep into the bowels of the building. They walked past the generators that supported the magma flows, the huge machines that pushed out the tufts of steam that erupted irregularly out in the club, and past the backstage people who made everything look and sound great. Luli stopped and exchanged pleasantries with a number of the stage crew before they finally reached the green rooms.

"Lu? Is that you?" A voice shouted from behind one of the closed doors.

"It's me, Vijay. Are you going to let me in?"

"What?" The door cracked open and Vijay's face poked out. He swung the door wide. "Come in! Come in!"

Vijay quickly shut the door and locked it behind them. He was a smallish man with a large gut, but with a spry step to his movement. His cyborg augments weren't overtly obvious to most people unlike Luli's. Technically, he was younger than she, and the technology of his time had been less invasive and extreme in appearance.

Luli looked on bemused, "Are you okay, Vijay? You seem nervous or something."

His smile brightened for a moment, "You know me too well. I'm still just a little jumpy since Palba's passing."

Anton muttered, "Murder can do that to a person."

Vijay turned and stared quizzically at Anton, "It sure can. Wait a minute. Is that you, Rabbit?" He searched Anton's face, "It is!" He beamed a smile at Luli, "I can't believe you're still traveling around with this pickney pirate!"

Luli chuckled as Anton blushed, "I most certainly am." She winked at Vijay, "You never know when you might need one on your side."

Vijay guffawed as he looked back and forth between the two of them. "Well, I'm glad to see that you guys are still shipping out together. How are Jacquie and Barney? Hopefully, everyone is well?"

"We're all just fine. Now, how are you doing these days?" Luli asked as she found herself a chair.

"Me? Oh, I'm just dandy." Vijay ran his hands through his short hair and the multiple ponytails that stuck out randomly sprang back into place.

"And eating very well it seems," Luli jested as she patted his belly. "How did you beat your weight stabilizer unit?"

The smile on his face fell, "It just stopped working one day. The tech is too damn old now. It's nigh impossible for me to find anyone who can fix it. Funny that. Age is finally catching up to me." He perked up and leered at her, "But you still look fantastic Ms. Qing! Those old belter technicians did good work."

She stuck her tongue out at him. "Well, when all you build is mining equipment, you build it to last."

Anton sat back and watched the two of them banter back and forth like the old friends they were. Vijay had made a good point. He hadn't really thought about it before but Luli's fabrication was noticeably different than the other deep spacers he had met. They all had that mechanized movement that was noticeable to varying degrees. But most of them could pass for regular humans if you didn't bother to look too closely. All except for Luli, that is. She looked more machine and less human in comparison, but her aura was so full of life that he hadn't noticed how different she truly was.

When he had first met her, he had been too awestruck by being in the presence of a deep spacer to be distracted by her machined mannerisms. And for a long time afterward, she had been the only deep spacer he ever knew. By the time he encountered other deep spacers, she was no longer an oddity, she was just Luli. As he sat back in the green room, he watched her movements and compared them to Vijay Bhatti's. Her sinuous movement was spattered through with micro-movements, like small jerks while Vijay's were more fluid, almost human.

Yet Luli was one of the most human

and upbeat beings he had ever known. Everything about her and everything she did screamed life. A contented smile bloomed across his face, "I love you, Luli. I hope you never change."

"What? Me change?" She went through a series of bodybuilder stances, "My makers built me to last. I am eternal!" She screwed her face up into a wrestler's mask and started laughing.

Vijay joined in her mirth and finally so did Anton. They barely heard the knock on the door for the five minutes to curtain warning.

***

Jacquie loosened the pistol in her holster as she marched purposefully toward the small bulbous ship. While it certainly wasn't the prettiest yacht, it looked well built. The surrounding area appeared deserted. She hadn't seen a single soul as she advanced toward the craft.

Jacquie raised her hand to knock on the airlock hatch and froze. The end of a gun barrel poked into her ribs and the comforting weight of her pistol disappeared from her hip. Her hands were pulled roughly behind her and a cord tightened around her wrists. A black-gloved fist tapped out a staccato pattern on the hatch. The airlock opened up and a small, strangely mustached man stood to the side. He looked her up and down, then thrust his head out and looked around. Without uttering a word, he waved them in and shut the hatch.

Jon Gray Lang

The interior of the vessel was bright, too bright. The light bounced off the oddly unsettling dark burgundy interior and glittered on the golden accents. Jacquie was roughly shoved forward and fell to her knees. Once she recovered her balance, she spied Barney hogtied near the back wall of the cabin. His face was puffy with bruises and cuts while the front of his shirt was sticky with blood and sweat. A growl rumbled in her throat but it was cut short when she was pulled her up by the wrists, spun her around and slammed against the wall.

She glared at the hired muscle in the refraction camo as the male Titan opened the hatch for him to leave. His outfit lightened to blend in with the early evening as the airlock closed behind him. Jacquie looked over her shoulder and stared into the swollen, bloodshot eyes of the man who had helped raise her. The man who had cared for her after her parents had been killed. The man who was the only family she had left from those days. For as long as she could remember, Barney had been in her life.

"What are you doing here, Jacq?" he mumbled past his split lips.

***

Anton had gone out to stand with the crowd in the club. In his opinion, it was the best place to watch the show and take part in the energy of the room. He had to elbow his way through some tough spots, but he managed to locate a place up front with a full, unobstructed view of the stage.

His cheer joined in the pandemonium from the rest of the crowd as Vijay stepped onto the stage. The musician waved as he hopped into his drum cage and beat out a quick tattoo. The crowd went wild. As the other band members entered the stage from both sides, Vijay introduced them to the crowd.

Vijay's inner showman came out strong, "We're excited to be here tonight in the Club Meltdown! We're electrified to be here with you! Now I don't want everyone to get too crazy tonight but have we got a special treat for you. She just flew in from the other side of the system and she's here for only one night! You know her! You love her! The incomparable Luli Qing!"

Luli stepped out onto the stage and light exploded around her. Anton didn't know how she did it, but she fairly glowed under the spotlight. The grin on her face as the crowd cheered for her went from ear to ear. She waved and then a new spotlight burst around the drummer. "Can we give some love to the amazing Vijay Bhatti? It's good to get to play with you again, old friend."

The crowd erupted into more applause when Vijay gave a quick countdown and the band launched into its opening song.

***

Jon Gray Lang

Derain watched as a dark figure pushed Jacquie into the yacht. He tried to stand, but Galena grabbed him by the shoulder and held him down. She glared at him, "First, we wait to see who else is out there."

Derain glared back but hunkered down behind her. The airlock hatch opened again and a single dark figure stepped out. As the hatch shut behind him, he blended into the darkness and quickly disappeared from view.

Derain could barely make out the feral grin on Galena's face in the poor light. Coldness spread through the center of his being as her eyes lit upon him.

"Are you ready to be prey, bounty hunter?"

***

Luli erupted into laughter as she collapsed onto the couch in Vijay's green room. Moments later Vijay backed into the room and stopped in the doorway. She heard him speak a few words with the rest of the band as they shuffled past to their green room. Then he closed the door and gazed at Luli sprawled out on the couch.

One of her legs was draped over the armrest while the other lay stretched out off the edge. Her arms were above her head and she glowed under the cheap lighting in the room.

Jon Gray Lang

"My, my.   Don't you look comfortable," he murmured.

"As comfortable as I can get!" She sat up and made room for him. "Thanks again for inviting me to join you on stage tonight. It's been a tough year. By Tom, I really needed that."

"Always, Lu. Always. But you know that." He got up and poured out a couple of drinks. He brought them over and handed her one, "Have you ever thought about settling? From personal experience, it's not too shabby. Steady work, getting to do what you want to do and all that."

"Don't you miss flying?" she asked. "Don't you miss seeing more than just this one world?"

"I've seen a lot more worlds than most people and so have you," he replied. "There isn't a whole lot of difference between them." He glanced toward her, "You should give it some thought."

Luli stretched, "I'm not ready to stop moving yet. But I'll take it under advisement."

Vijay chuckled though his eyes were downcast. He looked away from her, took a drink and exhaled slowly.

"Well, not to change the subject, but yeah, I'm changing it. What song are we using to begin the encore?" she asked.

He started, "Well, I thought we would...."

There was a knock at the door.

Jon Gray Lang

A quizzical expression crossed Vijay's face as he got up to answer it. He swung the door open and three men stood there, all in black. "What can I do for...?"

Luli jerked in alarm as Vijay screamed and fell to the floor. The three men burst into the room and the one in the middle clutched a shock stick. He jammed the shock stick into Vijay's chest and watched with glee as he convulsed. He kept at it until the cyborg stopped twitching.

Luli leapt up from the couch. A thug lunged at her, but she spun away with just enough room and time to avoid being caught. She yanked his shoulder and threw him across the room. The next man flew directly into her and knocked her over the couch.

"Get her!" shrieked the one with the shock stick.

She rolled away from the first assailant, who scrabbled to regain a handhold on her. The thug she had thrown across the room slowly rose up from the floor and pulled out a pistol. He fired a round into Luli's knee and the mechanism exploded outward. With a gasp, she crumpled forward.

The scruffy one behind the couch launched himself at her, knocked her onto her back and pinned her to the floor. The goon who had shot her leapt on top of her, too. They held her down as the man with the shock stick walked over and jammed the tip into her chest.

Jon Gray Lang

The shock paralyzed Luli's breathing and her servos bucked. He kept the shock stick against her until her servos failed and she collapsed. She looked on, trapped in her own body. There was no response from her chassis. She couldn't even close her eyes.

"That should keep her systems out of commission," grinned the brute with the shock stick. He pulled out a knife and threw it to one of the other men, "Get to it." He pulled out another knife and walked over to Vijay's prone body.

She watched in horror as he cut the skin along Vijay's scalp and moved the flap out of the way. He tapped the exposed skull with the handle of the knife and when he found what he was looking for, his eyes glittered. Luli couldn't look away. She couldn't close her eyes as the brute sawed into her longtime friend's neck. His fingers reached in and pried a bloody plate out of the way. Her own blood slowly dripped into one of her eyes as she saw his hand plunge into the cavity of Vijay's head and rip out his memory core.

Suddenly, the blood trickling from her scalp blinded her vision. Her body had completely shut down. Her systems were in a complete state of shock and there was absolutely nothing she could do about it. She felt nothing as her sensors had fried from the shock stick. Horrified, she wondered, "Is this the end?"

"Hey boss, this one is different," the goon above her grumbled. He continued to cut the

Jon Gray Lang

skin away from her skull.

The man pocketed Vijay's memory core and walked over to her. He reached down and smeared the blood away from her skull casing. It was unlike any of the other cyborg skulls he'd cracked. His man had cut the skin down to her mid-back and there didn't seem to be an access plate to her memory core anywhere.

He just stood over her and looked down, "Huh."

thirty

Gold Guns Girls

Derain did not like the Lieutenant's plan. In fact, he wasn't happy with it at all. He muttered to himself as he advanced toward the ugly sloop. He shook his head, "Titans and their eccentricities."

His great grandfather had told him tales of his dealings with them. Even though he had more knowledge about Titans than the average man, he just couldn't understand why they continued to do things in the way that they did.

The trek across the cool tarmac was taking much longer than he had anticipated. He quickened his pace to make up the difference. No matter how carefully he scanned the area, he still couldn't spot the door guard.

"He must be wearing some form of

adaptive camouflage," he muttered.

Derain's steps carried him past the berth marker sign. There was a slight noise behind him before he felt the end of a gun barrel press into the middle of his back.

There was an anguished cry behind him and the pressure from the barrel tip eased. He spun around just in time to see the Lieutenant's knife glint in the dark as it slashed across the assailant's neck. She caught the man as he crumpled and laid him out on the ground. The glare she gave Derain as she waved him forward caused him to step back.

He decided to glare back at her as he turned around and continued making his way toward the Cyclops. '*One down and who knows how many more to go,*' he thought.

He slowed as he came closer to the ship and scanned the gathering darkness for sentries. Only a minute would pass before he reached the hatch. A sudden scuffle on his left made him pause, but he ignored it and continued forward. The scuffle ended with a muffled grunt that was abruptly cut short.

Galena's hiss from behind caused Derain to square his shoulders and he picked up his pace. Shadows played haphazardly on the right side of the ships' exterior as a man garbed like the surrounding darkness stumbled out onto the tarmac and fell to the ground with a meaty thud. Two genorg soldiers melted out of the darkness and stood over the body. Agnes pulled her knife free from the guard's back and Carla slit his throat for good measure. Derain kept walking until he reached the airlock hatch. He stood there and waited, but no one else made a surprise appearance.

"Maybe there had only been three."

The six genorg soldiers, with Galena in the lead, stepped out of the darkness and arrayed themselves around Derain. He felt a little uneasy being surrounded by them.

Galena murmured, "Disappointing. I had expected more."

***

Anton finished his third libation of the night as he sat back and waited with the rest of the audience. Most of the band members had come out twice for instrumental encores, but neither Vijay nor Luli had returned to the stage. He knew these shows were important to Luli, so her absence for an encore struck him as being out of character. He set his empty glass down and strolled over to the bouncer.

The bouncer moved toward him and blocked the short staircase, "Access is restricted, sir."

"Hey. Remember me? I came in with Luli Qing."

She eyed him intently, then threw a quick glance both ways. With a little shuffle to the side, she created a small lane for Anton to pass through.

"Thanks," Anton said as he moved past her and headed back to the green rooms. He halted a couple members of Vijay's band as they headed back to the stage, "Hey guys. What's going on with Vijay and Luli?"

The bassist replied, "Haven't seen them since they left the stage, but the door to their room is locked. They might be in the middle of something if you catch my drift."

"Got it. Thanks for the heads up." Anton continued on his way to their room. When he finally got there, he hammered on the door. "Lu? You in there? You're missing your own show! Lu?"

There was only silence from the other side of the door. He grew worried and slammed into the door to break the lock. The third impact of his shoulder against the heavy door opened his stitches. But the plastic around the lock had begun to splinter. Blood trickled into the beltline of his pants as he leaned against the wall and gasped for breath. Strengthening his resolve, he crashed into the door again. As it flew open, he stumbled into the green room and haltingly came to a stop.

The couch had been flipped over and signs of a struggle were all over the place. Anton looked around wildly until he saw Vijay's body splayed out on the floor. There was a gaping hole in his head near a flap of skin that hung loosely from his skull. "What the hell happened in here?"

Anton cried out in a panic, "Lu! Are

you in here? Are you okay?" He searched the room in a frenzy and found her ukulele tossed haphazardly into a corner. He fell to his knees when he saw a lump of skin covered with her fine black hair in a pool of blood on the floor. "Lu? Please be alive! Luli?"

**

Lorin screamed, "Winston! How much longer before we can get off this backwater world?"

Jacquie's laughter echoed in the cabin. The priestess marched over and smacked her soundly across the face. The force of the blow was like the swing from a mallet and Jacquie's head crashed into the wall behind her.

Scorn, thick and heavy, burst from Lorin's lips, "Quiet your mouth, useless woman."

Jacquie spat blood from the open cut inside her cheek, "You aren't leaving this rock."

Barney tried to shush her.

She ignored him and threatened, "You'll never leave this mud ball if I have anything to do with it."

"We have about ten minutes, Ms. Basset."

"Ten minutes? More than enough time to break a person... and take their soul." Lorin sneered as she stopped in front of Jacquie and studied her quietly, "I see the weakness in you, merchant."

She shoved a balled-up rag into Barney's mouth and squatted just out of range of the Captain. "Do you want to know the story behind this vermin? On our world, things like it are not given rights. They aren't permitted to learn to read or to write. Their entire purpose for being lies within a very specific need and they are expected to fulfill it until it kills them."

She leaned back and pouted in mock sadness, "But this cur's family thought it was different. They ignored the teachings of the Ancestors and they taught it to read and write. They treated this worm like it had some value beyond its original purpose."

A grim smile crossed her face, "But we didn't know this, you see. We didn't understand the depth of the sins it had committed. Not until we took the truth from the mouths of its family. They had broken the tenets of our beliefs and their pleas fell on deaf ears. We dealt with them as we deal with all sinners. I consider myself fortunate to have personally sent them to the endless purgatory they had chosen. But I could not rest. The cause of their fall from the light was still free. This creature was still out there."

Jacquie noticed that Barney's eyes had sunken deep into his face and her expression darkened. Her eyes tightened and she glared back at the priestess.

Lorin chuckled at the naked anger on

the woman's face. "I once heard an intriguing story about a young girl, a young boy and a Titan who survived a pirate attack. It was a popular tale that was told on many a world." Her finger pressed against her lips, "Now, besides such an enigmatic set of heroes, what was so special about the tale? What made it unique? Oh yes, now I remember. The parents of that young girl had been brutally murdered by those same pirates. I understand that she cried for months." Her eyes bored into the captive woman, "Have you ever heard this story?"

Jacquie bit through each word, "If I were you, I would stop speaking now."

Lorin stood up and slowly paced back and forth. "Oh little one, I know this tale well, for I had a part to play in it. The hermaphrodite was still out there and that could not be allowed. It took us many decades to track down the ship that had taken the thankless androgyne from its world. So many vessels lost their crews in the search... until the name, Matilda was whispered in our ears."

Jacquie's eyes grew wide as she turned and stared at Barney in horror. His eyes squeezed shut and tears slowly trickled down his cheeks to the rag roughly tied around his mouth.

"I see that you know that name." Lorin smiled down at her, "We Titans are above all other humans, for we were molded by the hands of the Gods. We live long and we do not forget." She turned away from the prisoners, "It is a simple matter to find a single ship amongst thousands, amongst millions. All you need is time... time and mazuma, of course," frustration tinged her words. "It is a sad truth, but sometimes currency is needed to complete God's work."

Her eyes glittered as she spoke, "Do you finally comprehend how that thing beside you destroyed your life? I applaud you on your daring escape, but was not the cost too high? You lost so much because of this creature... the same animal that escaped long before you were ever born. The very sinner that shirked its God's given purpose. Can you imagine how different your existence would have been if it had never escaped its divine role in life?"

A quick series of raps on the hatch brought her up short. Winston looked back at Lorin and waited for her nod. He pressed the hatch controls and slid the airlock open. He stepped back in surprise as a man he didn't recognize and a horde of women, who all looked essentially the same, rushed through the opening.

Daphne and Anne pinned Winston against the ship's console. Derain lunged and smashed his pistol butt against the side of Lorin's head. She went down like a sack of grain. He pulled out his knife and cut through the bonds that held the two prisoners. Jacquie ripped the pistol out of his belt and pointed it at the Titan woman as she lay stunned on the deck.

Bitterness rang from Jacquie as she roared, "Didn't I say that you wouldn't leave this rock? And I do imagine how my life would have been different... every single day."

Jacquie pulled the trigger and the round tore into the woman's skull and spilled its contents onto the decking. She fired twice more into the body before she turned her attention to Winston. Again she pulled the trigger and the Titan spun. He slammed into a chair as the next two rounds thudded into his body. His last breath rattled through his throat.

Everyone stepped back. Jacquie's eyes were feral, raw and red. She stared wildly around the cabin before she regained a modicum of control. She threw Derain's pistol back to him and spat on the decking.

"Gather up the dead," she ordered. "We'll park this boat in the Matilda and deal with the carcasses off-planet."

She yanked Barney up and clamped onto his arm. Her eyes glared cruelly into his, "You've known this the whole time, haven't you. You knew you were responsible." She shoved him back to the floor, "I want you off my ship and out of my life."

Derain stared at her in shock. She dragged the dead male Titan away from the control, took the helm and began running a preflight check. Barney just lay there, too dazed to move. The bodies of the three mercenaries were dragged inside and the genorg soldiers melted away into the night. For those still aboard the little ship, it was a tight fit.

Galena's personal comm chimed and

Anton's voice exploded from it, "Lieutenant! Are you there? I'm trying to find the Captain!"

Galena glanced at Jacquie who glumly nodded. "She's here, Anton. What's up?"

Anton's choked voice came through, "We can't find a trace of her."

Galena's eyes widened, "Can't find who? Please repeat."

"Vijay was murdered and... and someone snatched Lu. I don't know who or why or where, but they took her!"

Fear and rage racked Jacquie's body. With grave concentration, she tuned out all the voices around her. She brought the little ship up and set its heading toward the Matilda. The only sound she couldn't completely dismiss was the heartbroken weeping of Barney in the background.

thirty-one

I'll Sail This Ship Alone

Galena stood in the cargo bay while Barney slowly brought down his few belongings. As soon as Anton had heard what had happened, he had taken up a collection of mazuma from everyone, except Jacquie. He embraced the engineer and forced him to take the currency. Hard tears streaked Barney's face as the young man strode to the lift and didn't look back.

Derain bid a brief farewell to Barney before he also headed toward the lift. He had to get back and check with his contacts on planet for any news about Luli. The hope was that someone might have heard a passing rumor about missing deep spacers or a boast about a kidnapping.

Barney headed toward the open cargo bay doors. Galena crossed her arms as he gazed upon the interior of the Matilda one last time. His heart and soul were integrated into the very fabric of this ship. It was a part of him as much as he was a part of it. Galena swallowed hard at the wrenching sadness in her chest, but the lump wouldn't budge.

"Well, this is goodbye, Lieutenant," Barney said sadly into the quiet.

She wiped at the wetness that formed at the corners of her eyes, "I won't say goodbye to you Barney. We will see each other again."

He smiled up at her, "When Jacq makes up her mind, she usually sticks to it. And in this case, I can't blame her. Her life would have been better if I hadn't been around. I'm responsible for the deaths of more people than I can bear to recall." He gave her a long hug, "You take good care of her, will you?"

He slung his gear over his shoulder and stoically trod out of the cargo bay into the night.

"This is not fair," she muttered. "In fact, this is bovine feces." She turned and stepped into the lift. Her resolve hardened as she rode it up to the top deck. Shouts, then silence rang down the hallway when she disembarked. Anton stomped past her with anger in every step and took the lift back down.

Galena found the Captain in the hallway near the airlock changing room. She had her back against one of the walls with her legs splayed out in front of her. In one hand she clutched a half-empty bottle while the other rested on her knee.

Jacquie's eyes stared deeply into the bottle of whiskey that had survived the death of her parents. She mused, "How many other bottles would I still have if he had never been on the Matilda?"

She took a hard swig, then rested her head against the bulkhead. The corners of her eyes were caked with the dried salt of the few tears that had escaped her. She still could taste their bitterness when she licked her lips.

"How had it come to this," Jacquie wondered. It hurt much more than she expected. The only reason her family was dead was as a byproduct of Barney's attempted abduction by his own cursed people.

Anton had vehemently disagreed with her sending Barney away and stormed off in anger. Derain, who had been more reticent than usual, had also left. And now Luli was missing. Only the Lieutenant, a person she wasn't sure she knew, was still on the ship with her.

"Do I truly know anyone, for that matter?" Jacquie muttered to herself.

She brought the bottle to her mouth only to see it violently knocked from her hand. Galena stood over her and she could feel the heat of the woman's anger.

"What are you doing?" Galena asked in a clipped tone.

Jacquie glared back, recovered the bottle and brought it back to her lips. The smack of Galena's hand against her cheek echoed in the hallway. Indifferent to the pain, Jacquie took another defiant swig of whiskey.

"What are you doing? Why did you send Barney away?" Galena screamed in her face. "He's a wanted man! He won't survive out there! How could you do this to him?"

Jacquie swung the bottle as hard as she could at Galena, but the Lieutenant deflected it and smacked her again. As her face reddened, Jacquie shouted back, "He's the reason my family is dead! He's why I have nothing! The very sight of him makes me want to puke!"

"He didn't kill them, Jacq! He had nothing to do with it!" Galena tried to reason with her, "He's as much an innocent in this as you were."

Jacquie shrugged her off and stood up slowly, with the bottle firmly clenched in her hand. "You wouldn't understand. You... you're not even real. You're a thing!"

"That's good! Get mad," Galena egged her on. "Might as well drive me away, right? Everyone else is gone. Then there'll be no one left here for you to give a shit about."

Jacquie continued, "You're just a drone! You wouldn't know what it is to be part of a family! To have a family! Never mind losing one!"

Galena's eyes grew hard and cold and her hands rolled into fists. "I wouldn't understand?

Tell me how I wouldn't understand. I'm not the one crying in a hallway like a poor lost babe."

Jacquie tensed and a growl escaped her when her face surged into a feral mask. She swung the bottle, the last physical reminder she had of her parents, and it shattered against the drone's head. She watched in horror as darkness enveloped the Lieutenant's eyes and her lips curled into a snarl.

The neck of the broken bottle fell from her fingers and shattered on the decking. "What am I doing? What have I done?"

Galena's swift movements were a blur. Jacquie felt the impact of an elbow to her face and a knee to her gut. She brought her knee up to block the impact, but she was too slow. Blow after blow rained down on her and she threw her hands up to defend herself.

A primal scream escaped Jacquie as she tucked her head down, pushed off the wall and slammed the genorg into the opposing wall. Galena grabbed her under the arm and spun her around. Her left fist and knee slammed into Jacquie's ribs. Galena's left elbow smashed into the woman's eye and split the skin. Jacquie struggled for breath as blood flow obstructed her vision. She barely saw the right fist that crashed into her temple. It stunned her and rendered her defenseless.

Galena grabbed her with both hands and threw her back into the wall. Jacquie slid down the wall and sucked in shallow breaths. Her trapped tears slid free. She looked up into the Lieutenant's twisted face and watched as the blackness in her eyes cleared to the strange, almost luminous, green that they normally were.

Galena stared down at this woman she had come to love, "I do understand, Jacq. Do you want to know why?" She scanned the hall before she turned to face her again, "You are my family. Barney is my family. This crew is my family and you're breaking us apart!"

She cupped Jacquie's chin in her hand, "You are tearing my family to pieces and you will be alone until you find the strength to put it back together." Galena stepped back and glared at her one last time before she turned away and strode down the hall.

Jacquie squinted through her bloodied vision as Galena walked away. The bottle fragments gleamed in the whiskey as the liquor pooled on the decking.

***

On his return from the airlock, Derain discovered broken glass in the hall and the air was sticky with whiskey. He continued on his way to the bridge. Once he was there, he kept an eye on the cargo door monitor and waited. Eventually, he saw Anton wave and nod to the camera before he disappeared into the Matilda. He keyed the comm to the cargo bay, "Might as well close her up, Rabbit."

Jon Gray Lang

The air pressure changed as someone entered the bridge. He turned slowly and a beaten and bloodied Jacquie stood alone in the hatch. He looked over, but kept his distance and didn't say a word. She just stood there. It hurt to see her like this. After a while, he asked, "Are you alright?"

She felt the concern that leaked through his guardedness. Jacquie closed her good eye and drew in a solid breath before she released it in a whoosh. She gazed back at him and asked, "Is Anton aboard?"

After he nodded, she relaxed a fraction, "Good. We're going after Luli." The steel of her nature came through in her words, "And I don't care who has to be paid off, hurt or broken to give us a lead. Nothing will stop us from finding her. Nothing."

thirty-two

Le Dèserteur

The walk across the black tarmac was long, but she still lived. There was energy in every step she took that only increased as she grew closer to her destination. Another chance had been given, another choice had been made and she had jumped at it.

She stretched her legs and shifted the heavy pack on her back. Everything she owned fit into one small bag, but this time she carried it to a renewed future. Her steps slowed at the sign for Berth 789-G. With a left turn at the next branch, she caught sight of her new home, her new post. That is if the crew would have her.

The Independence glittered in the light of the two suns like a beacon of hope. The name alone made her smile. She stepped through

Jon Gray Lang

the airlock and into the middle of the bay of this strange vessel. She felt eyes burn into her from every direction. She came to a halt and waited as two genorg soldiers approached from the side. They stopped in front of her and she nodded to them both.

"You must be Delta and Gamma," Rosa stated. "No? Delta and Omega then?"

The two women nodded, but their eyes remained hard. Rosa reached into her jacket and the audible clicks from multiple weapons echoed in the cargo bay. She slowed down her motions and brought out a folded piece of paper. A hand reached around her and pulled it free from her fingers. This third woman stepped around her and joined the other two.

"Aah. You must be Gamma." Rosa stuck out her hand, "Pleased to meet you again."

The three genorg commanders ignored her as they read the slip of paper. Disbelief reigned when Delta held it out to her, "What is this?"

Rosa rocked on her heels and placed her hands behind her back. "Those are orders from your new employer. The cargo you will be delivering should arrive within the hour. I have been hired on as your pilot, for now."

"This states you are in command," said Omega.

Rosa leaned over and read the note, "Nominally in charge." She pointed to the section,

"Really, I am just your pilot. Anytime this bird is off the ground, that would put me in charge." Her hand dropped to her side and she leaned back. "Anytime we're on the ground, you would be in charge." She spread her arms out, "You all would be in charge." Mr. Leon had humorously mentioned that this would be a tough sell.

She could understand their anger. These women were not happy that their status had just changed. But the rest of her existence hinged on this moment. Her fate rested in the hands of these women. Their decision would either grant her life or be a warrant for her death. "Permission to come aboard?"

Delta crumpled up the piece of paper. "Granted," she intoned.

"True independence is a myth, ladies," Rosa declared to her new shipmates. "And hope is a terrible thing," she muttered to herself.

thirty-three

The Songs for the Chapter Titles

As it was in the first book so it is in the second. All the chapter names are actually song titles and are part of Ms. Luli Qing's performances. These songs helped set the mood for each chapter, but in some cases, only certain versions were selected. If you are interested, here they are:

☐ In the Hole - Phillip Roebuck
☐ 2Wicky - Hooverphonic
☐ Burial on the Presidio Banks - This Will Destroy You
☐ Maps - Yeah Yeah Yeahs
☐ More Heat than Light - The Veils
☐ Dream On - Depeche Mode
☐ Wayfaring Stranger - David Eugene Edwards
☐ Army of Me - Bjork

Jon Gray Lang

- ☐ Tracks of My Tears - Smokey Robinson & the Miracles
- ☐ Full Moon - Pavlo
- ☐ Way Out There - Lord Huron
- ☐ Black Sun - Death Cab for Cutie
- ☐ Insane in the Brain - Cypress Hill
- ☐ Amen - Rocco Deluca
- ☐ Ringo Bushi - The Yoshida Brothers
- ☐ Undone in Sorrow - Crooked Still
- ☐ Old Ship of Mine - Old Tex Morton
- ☐ Bold Fisherman - Ed McCurdy
- ☐ Another Saturday Night - Sam Cooke
- ☐ In the Aeroplane Over the Sea - Neutral Milk Hotel
- ☐ Blood & Wine - Dustin Kenstrue
- ☐ You on the Run - Black Angels
- ☐ Don't You Evah – Spoon
- ☐ Eye of Demand - Trevor Green
- ☐ An Honest Mistake - The Bravery
- ☐ Gypsies, Tramps and Thieves- Cher
- ☐ Life's Been Good - Joe Walsh
- ☐ Gaily the Troubadour - Old Folk Song
- ☐ Stuck in the Middle - Stealers Wheel
- ☐ Gold Guns Girls - Metric
- ☐ I'll Sail This Ship Alone - Patsy Cline
- ☐ Le Déserteur - Boris Vian

The title of the book is also a song:
- ☐ Twistin' Matilda - Jimmy Soul

Jon Gray Lang

I hope you enjoyed hanging out with the crew of the Matilda.   The Matilda's story continues in Black Matilda!

Jon Gray Lang

***

About the Author

Jon Gray Lang was born in Australia before being hastily relocated to the United States where he wrote a handful of screenplays, shot a few films, and even threw his hat into the acting ring. But with a life-long love of science fiction, it was only a matter of time before he bit the novel writing bullet and wrote the award-winning five book science fiction series, Saga of a Space Freighter. When he's not typing away at the keyboard, he's busy fighting with rapiers, skiing the Rockies, or banging out tunes on a ukulele... just not all at once... No matter how hard he tries.

Please follow him on:

JonGrayLang.com
facebook.com/JonGrayLang
twitter.com/Jon_Gray_Lang
instagram.com/jongraylang

<<<<>>>>

Jon Gray Lang